THE DEATH BRINGERS

A TEAM REAPER THRILLER

THE CABAL BOOK 2

BRENT TOWNS

WOLFPACK PUBLISHING
— EST 2013 —

WOLFPACK PUBLISHING
— EST 2013 —

Published in the United States by Wolfpack Publishing, Las Vegas

Wolfpack Publishing
6032 Wheat Penny Avenue
Las Vegas, NV 89122

wolfpackpublishing.com

Paperback ISBN: 978-1-64734-672-0
eBook ISBN: 978-1-64734-671-3

THE DEATH BRINGERS

Worldwide Drug Initiative

General Mary Thurston: Bravo
Luis Ferrero: Zero
Carlos Arenas: Zero-One

Team Reaper

John "Reaper" Kane: Reaper One
Cara Billings: Reaper Two
Raymond "Knocker" Jensen: Reaper Three
Axel "Axe" Burton: Reaper Four
Richard "Brick" Peters: Reaper Five

Bravo Team

Brooke Reynolds: Bravo One
Pete Traynor: Bravo Two
Pete Teller: Bravo Three
Sam "Slick" Swift: Bravo Four
Doctor Rosanna Morales

SEALs

Borden Hunt: Scimitar
Mike Oil: Popeye
Rucker

Others

General Hank Jones
Rear Admiral Alexander Joseph
Striker
Anvil
Mr. White
CIA Director Paul Brewer
Speaker of the House Clarissa Rhodes
President Richard Nelson

CHAPTER 1

Aleppo, Syria

The team had been in some shitholes before, but this was about the worst of them. What had once been a beautiful city was now in ruins: bombed-out buildings, craters, wrecked vehicles, and bullet holes in sandstone walls. The ravages of war were evident everywhere, and in the middle of it all was Team Reaper.

"Zero, this is Reaper One. Target house in sight."

"Good copy, Reaper One," came the reply from Luis Ferrero.

The term "house" in reference to the building might have been a bit of a stretch since the top part was mostly destroyed. It had once been a three-floor building, but the war had made short work of it, and its best days were now long behind it.

John "Reaper" Kane, six-four, dark hair, Reaper

tattoo on his back, signaled his second in command, Cara Billings, forward. "What's up?"

Cara was in her mid-thirties, lean with short dark hair. She was also the team's sniper, and at that moment, Kane had a job for her. "Set up across the street and keep an eye out. You should be able to provide good cover from there."

She looked to her right at the damaged three-floor structure. "It'll do," she agreed with a nod.

As she ran across the street, Kane turned to the rest of his team. "You all ready?"

"Let's get it done," Knocker Jensen growled with his typical British accent. "I'm sick of standing around playing with my dobber."

Knocker was ex-SAS from 22 Squadron, with fifteen years in the service. He was solidly built, with dark hair and a neatly trimmed beard.

"Your fucking *what?*" Axel "Axe" Burton asked the former SAS man.

Knocker's speech confused the hell out of the man standing next to him. He turned to him and grinned at the big ex-recon Marine. "My dick, Axel me old mate."

"Why didn't you just say so?"

"Because I like yanking yours."

"Shit."

Each team member was dressed in full combat gear: body armor, webbing with extra ammunition and grenades, ballistic helmets, and suppressed

Heckler & Koch 416s and SIG Sauer M17 handguns, except for Cara, who carried an M110A1
CSASS sniper system. At the rear of the small
column came Brick Peters, their combat medic. He
was a big ex-SEAL with a shaved head, a beard, and
a number of tattoos. He'd come to the team from
the private sector.

A few moments later, a voice came over their
comms. "Reaper Two in position."

"Knocker, you're breacher. Lead out," Kane ordered.

"Thought you'd never ask," the man said and
hurried toward the building, sweeping from his
twelve to his three o'clock.

Falling in behind him, the others followed until
they reached the target building and paused on
either side of the door. Knocker reached out and
tried it but found it locked. This was Kane's least
favorite part—daylight with a locked door, leaving
them exposed.

"Reaper One, this is Zero-One, copy?"

Zero-One was Carlos Arenas in his new assign-
ment. Since being wounded in an artillery strike in
Afghanistan, he'd given up his role in the field as
Reaper Three to become part of Bravo team as an
operational planner.

"Copy, Zero-One."

"*Amigo*, the hair on the back of my neck is standing up. Watch your six."

Before joining the Worldwide Drug Initiative, Carlos had been in charge of a Mexican Special Forces team and had a lot of experience with operations like this. He also had a sixth sense about trouble.

The plan on paper was simple, as much as inserting a team into war-torn Syria and extracting them could be regarded as such. The op consisted of hitting the objective and extracting the HVT supposedly contained within. Abbas al-Kassar was a terrorist first and foremost, which would normally be assigned to the likes of a SEAL team. However, because he made the bulk of his money selling cocaine, the mission landed squarely in the lap of the WDI.

According to the latest intel, the target was supposedly in the building, even though there had not been a PID or positive identification. In fact, the team was going in blind apart from the limited intel they had managed to gather themselves.

Knocker set the breaching charge and stepped to the right along the solid wall. "All clear?"

"Clear," Kane confirmed.

"Fire in the hole," the Brit said and blew the charge.

The team swept into the rundown building and methodically began clearing the rooms. Shortly after their insertion, it became evident to Kane that something was wrong. They met no resistance, although the building was supposed to have at least four fighting-age males onsite. Within minutes, the team called all clear. Each intact room they had cleared was empty.

Knocker growled, "This is a dog's fucking dinner, this is."

"What he said, Reaper," Axe added by way of agreement.

"Split up," Kane ordered them. "Search everything."

As they did so, Kane got on his comms. "Zero, copy?"

"Read you Lima Charlie, Reaper One."

"There's no one here, Luis. The intel was fucked up."

"We were assured it was good, Reaper. It came straight from Brewer."

Paul Brewer was the new director of the Central Intelligence Agency, who'd been appointed after the murder of Melissa Smith by the Cabal. "How sure are we about him, Zero?"

"What are you saying, Reaper One?" The question came from the WDI commander, General Mary Thurston.

"I'm saying the intel was shit, ma'am. There is no one here, and it looks as though there hasn't been here for a good while."

"And?"

"And we don't know Brewer from Adam."

There it was—the Sword of Damocles that had

been hanging over them for the past two months, just waiting to fall. "Wait one, Reaper," Thurston ordered.

"Yes, ma'am."

Bravo Team, Incirlik, Turkey

General Mary Thurston made sure she couldn't be heard over her comms before she turned to Luis Ferrero and asked, "Is he right? Could this be the start of something? God knows they're out on a limb right now."

Thurston was a competent officer in her early forties. She had a lithe build and bore a striking resemblance to the actress Rhona Mitra, with her long dark hair and brown eyes.

Ferrero, on the other hand, had been career DEA when he'd founded the small team that would become the WDI. He was in his late forties, solidly built and average height, with graying hair. He was Thurston's second in command and the operations commander.

He shrugged. "I don't know, Mary."

"We need to find out," she snapped. "Carlos."

Arenas ran a hand through his short-cropped black hair before putting his headset back on. He was in his late thirties, and this was only his second mission since joining Bravo. When he spoke, his voice was short and clipped. "I want full ISR coverage *now*. Slick, get me a satellite. Bravo One, I want you to do a wide sweep of the area immediately."

Slick was the first to answer. The red-headed computer tech was an integral part of the team, whose skills and commitment level they relied on heavily when they were both in and out of the field. "On it, Carlos."

"Zero-One, we're commencing a wider sweep now," Brook Reynolds replied. She was the team UAV pilot in charge of the MQ-1C Gray Eagle they had orbiting overhead at five thousand meters.

Reynolds was tall—six-two without her boots on. She too had long dark hair and could double in the field when required.

Beside her sat Master Sergeant Pete Teller, who had come aboard from the US Air Force as Reynolds' second seat. A big man with broad shoulders, he had an uncanny ability to interpret data as it came through.

"I want you to bring up the UAV feed on the screen," Arenas ordered. "Switch from helmet cams."

The team's helmet cams were a new thing for them. Although they had been utilized by Special Forces for a long time, Team Reaper had done without them. Now, at the general's insistence, they wore them.

The benefit of operating in daylight was that the feed from the UAV camera was a lot clearer. Not that the view was anything to write home about because a good chunk of that part of Aleppo was pretty much destroyed. Hell, most of the city was destroyed.

"There," Arenas snapped before anyone could speak. "Six vehicles inbound. Get in close on them."

"Zero, we have a problem," Swift called across the hangar to where the team had their base of operations set up.

"What is it, Slick?" Ferrero asked.

"There's already a satellite tasked over North Africa."

"What do you mean, already?"

"Someone is watching the operation, and it isn't us."

Alarm sprang to Thurston's face. "Track that feed *now*, Slick."

"Yes, ma'am."

"Reaper One, copy?" Thurston said urgently into her comms.

She waited for a reply, but none came.

"Reaper One, this is Bravo, do you read? Over."
Still no reply.

"Slick, are we being jammed?" she snapped.

"I'll just check, ma'am."

Thurston looked at Arenas and then the screen. The camera on the UAV, which was zooming in on the incoming vehicles, suddenly went blank.

"What the hell?" Reynolds blurted. "Ma'am, I've lost all power."

"Me too," called Swift.

"Check it, Slick. Get it back up."

"Yes, ma'am."

The computer tech disappeared into the room at the rear where their servers had been set up. Meanwhile, the rest were virtually useless.

Suddenly Peter Traynor appeared, coming through the entrance of the hangar with a strange expression on his face. Thurston knew something was wrong when behind him appeared five soldiers with MP armbands on their sleeves. Thurston frowned. "What's going on?"

"You're all under arrest," the lead man said.

"The hell we are. We're in the middle of a fucking mission."

Another man walked through the door. He was big, broad-shouldered, and had dark hair. Colonel Grady Brooks was the American commanding officer of Incirlik Air Force Base. "That mission has been canceled, General."

"You'd better have a good reason, Mister," she snarled. "I've got people on the ground in a hostile fucking environment, and they've got inbound almost on top of them."

"I'm sorry, General. I have my orders."

"What about my people?"

"Sorry, General. I have my orders," he repeated.

The realization that her team was about to be left in the field with no plan for extraction hit her. They were going to be sacrificed for some reason she knew nothing about. "Luis, get me General Jones."

"I'm afraid that won't be possible, General," a new voice said.

Thurston's eyes widened as CIA Director Paul Brewer appeared. He had a smug expression on his face. "You'll all be in custody for a while before you get the option of a phone call."

"What for?" Ferrero asked.

"A bombing took place in a market in Ankara yesterday. At first, it was thought that extremists had set off a car bomb. Further investigation tells a different story: it was caused by a Hellfire missile. That missile was fired from an MQ-1C Gray Eagle. See where I'm going with this?"

Thurston did. "You fucking traitorous bastard," she hissed vehemently.

He turned to the colonel. "Take them away and make sure they talk to no one. They'll be transferred to Ankara later today."

Brooks looked around the hangar. "Where's the other one?"

"What?" Brewer asked.

"The other one. There's another one. The computer tech."

"Well, find him, damn it."

Brooks nodded, and two of the MPs began the search for Swift. They wouldn't find him since he'd seen what was happening and was already in the wind.

Aleppo, Syria

"Zero, do you copy?"

Nothing.

Kane tried again. "Zero, do you copy?"

"Nothing."

"All callsigns, copy?"

This time he got an answer. "OK, listen up. For some reason, Bravo has gone dark. I have no idea why, but that's it in a nutshell. We need to get moving to the extract zone."

"Hey, Reaper," Brick said over the comms. "I've got a tunnel in the basement."

Normally Kane would have investigated, but he had the feeling something was coming down the pipe, and it wasn't good. "Leave it, Brick. Everyone rally on me. Cara, how are we looking?'

"Wait one, Reaper."

"What's going on, Reaper Two?"

"We've got a small convoy inbound to our position."

"Shit. How many vehicles, Cara?"

"Looks like six."

"Hold your position, Reaper Two. Let's see what they're up to."

"Roger that."

"All callsigns, we've got incoming tangos. Take up defensive positions and wait for my command."

"You get the feeling we've been fucked over, Reaper?" asked Axe.

"Yeah, and then some. Set up that SAW at the front."

"Roger that."

The White House, Washington, DC
-7 Hours

President Jack Carter was looking at his watch when his Secret Service detail burst into the Oval Office. He was in a meeting with his advisors about Russian troops being moved to the Ukraine border and the response they would make to try to counteract it.

Carter was a grumpy man in his late sixties with gray hair, and when his meeting was interrupted by his detail, he wasn't about to be all mellow about it. "What the fuck are you boys doing?" he snarled.

"I'm sorry, Mister President, but we have to move you to the bunker right away, sir," the lead officer replied hurriedly.

"Why, damn it?"

"There has been a threat made against your life, sir."

"By who, damn it?"

"I'll tell you on the way, sir."

"You'll tell me now."

"General Hank Jones, sir."

Carter opened his mouth to say something but found himself on his feet without any effort on his part. He was rushed from the room in a crush of suited men. All of the president's advisors came to their feet except for one—a blue-eyed, gray-haired man wearing a rear admiral's dress whites. Alexander Joseph was still trying to process what he'd heard when voices were raised and two shots rang out.

He came to his feet and rushed out of the office against the tide of advisors streaming the other way, away from the gunfire. When he reached the scene, he stopped and looked down in horror. The lead Secret Service officer lay on the floor with what looked to be a self-inflicted gunshot wound. Beside him, with a bullet hole in the side of his head, lay President Jack Carter.

Thoughts whirled through Joseph's mind as he tried to make sense of what had just happened. They came down to one that made him reach into his pocket for his cell. He hurriedly punched in a number and waited for the answer, then he said, "Get him underground *now.*"

Appalachian Mountains, Maine

"Give me one good reason why the hell I should leave here, Chief? And make it a *damn* good one," General

Hank Jones demanded. He stood in the center of the cabin with his hands on his hips, challenging Navy SEAL Chief Borden Hunt to try to get him out the door.

Hank Jones was a big man in his late sixties who looked a lot like a former US general by the name of Norman Schwarzkopf, Jr. He'd served in Vietnam as part of the 75th Rangers toward the end of the war before coming home, then stayed in and worked his way up the chain to where he was today: Chairman of the Joint Chiefs.

Hunt, codename "Scimitar," a veteran of the teams, was in no mood to take the general's shit. He was a man of average height and build and had dark hair. This was his detail, and what he said was law. As he shrugged into his tactical vest, he stared into the general's eyes and said, "Because I fucking said so…sir. Now get your ass in gear."

Jones frowned, "All right, Chief, we'll do it your way."

Hunt nodded and picked up his M4A1 carbine and said into his comms, "Check in."

"Popeye is all clear."

"Rucker all clear."

"Good copy, all clear."

Hunt looked at Jones. "We're good to go, General. I'll escort you to the SUV, and then we'll take the back roads out of here."

"So much for a quiet fishing trip," he growled.

"You ready?"

"Let's get it over and done with. It's probably a false alarm."

Somehow, deep down, he knew that wasn't the case. A feeling of dread had surfaced when Hunt had taken the call from Alex Joseph, and it hadn't gone away.

They both walked toward the door of the cabin and stopped. Hunt said, "We're coming out."

The reply that came back from Mike "Popeye" Oil wasn't what he expected. "Scimitar, hold. I say again, hold. We've got incoming. Rucker falls back to the cabin."

"Copy that."

Hunt said, "Popeye, rig for silent running."

"Roger, Boss."

The SEAL chief turned to Jones. "We're staying here for the moment. We've got incoming. Go to the kitchen and hunker down there."

Jones frowned, and Hunt nodded. He took out his Heckler and Koch HK45C from its thigh holster and handed it over. "There's one in the pipe, General."

"Thanks, Chief."

Hunt's phone rang and he cursed. Now was not the time. "Not now, Admiral," Hunt growled.

"What's going on, Scimitar?" Joseph snapped back.

"We've inbound tangos."

"Damn it, they're really making a move. You have

to get Hank out of there, Bord. It's all gone to shit."

"What has?"

"Jack Carter was just assassinated by one of his detail, and Hank Jones had been implicated."

"The Cabal?"

The door to the cabin opened, and Rucker slipped in. He was a solid operator with brown hair who stood six-one. Hunt waved him in.

"I'd say so, Chief," Joseph said. "Just do what you can to get him out and then take him to Zulu Six. Copy?"

"Lima Charlie, sir. I'll reach out when I can."

The call disconnected, and Hunt stared at Rucker. "Take the rear."

"On it."

"Popeye, talk to me."

"We have four SUVs incoming, Bord. They're black. If I had to guess, those fuckers are CIA, or my ass doesn't point toward the ground."

"Find a good hide, Pop," Hunt ordered. "If something goes down, reach out and touch those assholes."

"Count on it, Chief."

Unlike Hunt and Rucker, Popeye's personal weapon was a Heckler and Koch 417. It fired a 7.62 round and doubled as a Designated Marksman Weapon. His had the twenty-inch barrel, which meant he could pick off anyone within eight hundred meters.

The SUVs appeared, four in a line. Stopping abruptly in a cloud of dust, they disgorged approximately twelve men, all dressed in tactical gear, who took refuge behind their vehicles. All except one, who stood out in the open—a tall man with red hair.

"Chief, I've got twelve tangos. They're either CIA or private contractors."

"I've got them, Pop," Hunt replied.

The red-headed man took a deep breath and shouted, "We're here for General Jones. He's wanted for the assassination of the President."

"What the hell is he talking about?" Jones snapped from where he stood in the doorway to the kitchen.

"Damn it, General," Hunt growled. "Get down."

"Tell me what's going on, Chief."

"The admiral told me Jack Carter was assassinated and that you were implicated. He's ordered me to get you out of here to Zulu Six."

"The President is dead?" Jones asked in disbelief, shaking his head.

"Yes, sir, I'll tell you about it later."

"What the fuck is Zulu Six?"

"Alleghenies. The SEALs had an old training camp up there years ago for escape and evasion maneuvers."

"Can you hear me in there?"

Hunt looked at Jones. "I'll handle this. You just get ready to do as I tell you."

"All right, Chief. I'm all yours."

Hunt turned back toward the door and said, "Get ready, Pop. I'm coming out."

CHAPTER 2

Washington, DC

The encrypted satellite phone buzzed and was answered almost immediately. The voice on the other end said, "It's done. The teams are in play. We should have a result soon."

"And what about your end, Paul?"

"Incirlik is secure. Do we need another team to take care of the VP?"

"No, he can be manipulated. There will be a meeting soon, and he will be sworn in. I wasn't sure how this would go with you out of the country, but it looks as though there was nothing to worry about."

"As I said it would."

"Yes, you did. With Richard as president, I will be able to put the rest of the plan into action. With Hank Jones out of the way and Thomas as chairman, we will be able to start deploying troops to Europe to meet the Russian aggression."

"The rest of the leaders will be pleased."

"Of course, they will be. Once again, America will rise to the occasion and come to their defense. Only this time, there will be no stopping until the corrupt communist regime is suppressed for good. We'll show them we can't be walked over."

"Congratulations, Ares."

The call disconnected.

Appalachian Mountains, Maine

Hunt stepped out onto the cabin's veranda and stopped, all too aware that at any point, one of the shooters before him could drop him on the spot. He said in a low voice, "Anyone of these asshole sneezes, Pop, you kill him."

"Roger that."

"Who are you, and what do you want?" Hunt called.

"Are you Hunt?" the red-headed man called back.

"You have me at a disadvantage, friend."

The man stared at the chief, aware that the SEAL still had a hand on his M4 and could easily raise it to fire at any time. "The name is White. I'm here on behalf of the government."

Hunt knew he was lying, which made him think

these guys were CIA. "You always bring this much backup with you when you come visiting?"

White looked at his men. "Only when it's important."

"Must be mighty important then."

"Matter of life and death," White replied.

"Really?"

"Yes, we're here to get the general. There's an imminent threat, and his life may be in danger."

"Funny how you're here to move the general to safety, and all of your weapons are pointed at the cabin. Any asshole who knows what he's doing would set up a perimeter."

White gave Hunt a mirthless smile and said, "My bad."

"Do it, Pop."

The crack of the 417 could be heard as it filtered through the trees surrounding the cabin. The head of a shooter seemed to explode as a 7.62 round punched into it, spraying gore over the man standing next to him.

Hunt moved to the nearest upright to use it for cover, brought his M4 up, and started picking targets as best he could. He said into his comms, "Rucker, out front."

"On my way."

The first shot from Popeye threw chaos into the newcomers behind the SUV, who were surprised there was a new and unexpected threat. The second shot from the 417 killed another man, and the third wounded one more.

White shouted at his men, who turned to face the new danger, leaving Hunt free to begin dealing his own brand of death. His first shot killed a target who was firing toward Popeye's position. The 5.56 round from the M4 punched into the shooter's head just above his ear. Flipping the selector to auto, Hunt began raking the vehicles with steady gunfire, rendering them useless.

"Rucker, cover me."

Hunt left his position and fell back through the door into the cabin. Rucker had taken up position at the window and was firing at a shooter near the second SUV.

Once inside the cabin, Hunt moved to the second window and peered out. He could see White trying to rally his men, who were still firing wildly in all directions.

"Pop, you all good?"

Hunt could hear the crack of rounds through the comms when the SEAL spoke. "Yeah, I'm good. These guys must be Boy Scouts or something because they can't shoot for shit."

"Fall back to the rear of the cabin. We'll meet you out there."

"Roger that."

"Rucker, you want to leave these guys a little surprise before we go?"

"On it, Boss."

While Rucker went to work, Hunt kept up his fire on the CIA kill team. A few minutes later, Rucker said, "We're good to go."

"All right, fall back. Take the general with you."

"Copy that."

Rucker disappeared into the kitchen. While he did that, Hunt blew off a second magazine in the shooters' direction, dropped it out, replaced it with a fresh one, fired three more shots, and then pulled back.

As he went out the rear door, he saw Rucker and the general in front of him. Rucker had picked up his unit one pack, which contained all the medical supplies he might require as the combat medic.

He followed them into the trees and caught up to them and Popeye. Looking at the SEAL sniper, he said, "Take point, Pop. We're going to Zulu Six."

"That's a long walk, Chief," Popeye pointed out.

Hunt gave him a grim smile. "I have no plans to walk."

"Copy that."

"General, are you OK?"

"Point me in the right direction and give me someone to shoot, Chief."

"Let's go, sir."

"Hold your fire!" White shouted above the din. "What the fuck? I thought you guys were frigging trained operators. Jesus Christ."

The echoes eventually subsided as they dissipated amongst the trees. The tall pines seemed to devour the noise as it filtered through the dappled light they permitted to hit the ground. The CIA man picked out two shooters. "You and you, go and search the cabin."

They gave him a strange look.

"Oh, for crying out loud. They're not in there, or they'd be shooting at you."

White's temperament matched his red hair. He also had freckles on his pale face, and blue eyes to go with them. He topped the measuring stick at six-two, and being an ex-serviceman, had done two tours of Iraq, three of Afghanistan, and one in Nigeria with a small unit tasked to help Nigerian soldiers root out ISWA terrorists.

After finishing that tour, the CIA had come knocking. His agreement had brought him into the fold to join the covert world, where the darkest of shadows was the place to live. He'd liked it; enjoyed it, in fact. There were no rules, just results.

Then, after three years of living and working in the shadows, he had been approached by a man who appeared to be just as shady as his own world. The man had asked, "Are you a patriot, Mister White?"

White had started to reply, "My name—"

"No, I don't need to know your name. To me, you're Mister White."

White had nodded. After listening to the man's spiel, he'd given his answer. That was how he'd become the commander of one of the Cabal's dark units. One of many.

The two operators went inside the cabin. There was movement beside White, who turned to the man and asked, "How many?"

"Six."

"Fuck me, what the hell—"

BOOM!

The interior of the cabin exploded in an orange fireball that lifted the roof and sent wooden splinters scything through the air. White ducked instinctively and then looked around to see the cabin already engulfed in flame. He cursed violently and kicked at the ground like a child. He'd come here with twelve men, including himself. There were only four left.

To say that his boss would not be happy was an understatement, especially when he told him their target had evaded their net.

––––––––

Aleppo, Syria

Six Humvees and what looked to be about twenty shooters, including the ones on the three 50-caliber machine guns, approached the team. Kane grew nervous. "Reaper Two, copy?"

"Read you Lima Charlie, Reaper One." Cara's voice was low, almost hushed.

"You got twenty shooters?"

"Roger that."

"Anyone get the feeling this is about to go ass over tits?" Knocker asked through his comms.

"If you mean 'down the shitter,' you're right," Axe growled.

"Axel, mate, you know your onions."

Kane smiled. Even though he couldn't see the expression on Axe's face, he could imagine it. Then he heard the big ex-Marine say, "Fucking what?"

"All right, you two," Kane interrupted. "Get your heads in the game."

"Let's just waste these asshats, Reaper," Knocker growled into his comms. "Let the Death Bringers loose."

"Just hold your fire for the moment while we see what these guys want."

Cara's hushed voice came over the comms. "Reaper, I can hear these guys talking. They're French."

"What the hell are French—"

"Reaper One, this is Bravo Four. Copy?"

Kane stopped. There was something about the hushed voice over the comms that set him on edge. "Copy, Bravo Four."

"Listen, I don't have much time. Something is

wrong. The rest of the team has just been taken into custody by the director of the CIA."

"He's there at Incirlik?"

"Yes. From what I overheard, it has something to do with a bombing—" A crackle interfered with the comms.

"Say again your last, Bravo Four."

Swift's voice came clear once more. "They're jamming our frequencies, and I have to keep working around it. I'll meet you in Mersin, Turkey."

"What the hell is going on, Slick?" Kane demanded.

"Just go to Mersin. By the way, if you don't already know, you have inbound tangos."

"They're here. French mercenaries would be my guess."

"Get out and run for the border, Reaper. This is all bad."

"Is it the Cabal?" Kane asked

"I don't know."

"We'll see you there, Bravo Four. Wherever 'there' is."

"I'll reach out if I can."

"Good luck, Slick."

"You too, Reaper."

"You all get that?" Kane asked his team.

They all acknowledged the transmission. "Reaper," said Knocker, "are we going to shit or get off the pot?"

"We don't know if they're hostile, Knocker," Kane reminded him.

"Uh-huh," the SAS man said and stood, framed by what had once been a window. "Oi, frog-fucker, you friendly or a fucking John Thomas?"

One of the French mercenaries turned around and opened fire with a FAMAS F1 assault rifle. His actions were quickly followed by others. To top that off, the 50s opened fire with their familiar CHUG-CHUG-CHUG, and holes as big as melons began to open in the target building's walls.

"What the hell did you say to him, Knocker?" Axe growled as he opened fire with the M249 SAW.

"I guess he didn't like me calling him a dick, Axe."

"Are you sure it wasn't the 'frog-fucker' part?" Brick asked.

"Could have been that, I suppose," the SAS man agreed as he shot a mercenary.

"What did you boys do over there?" Cara asked over the comms.

"The wanker couldn't take a joke," Knocker told her.

"What joke was that?"

"I called him a male appendage."

"I see."

Kane said, "Reaper Two, knock out those damned fifties."

"Roger that."

From where she was, Cara sighted on the first target with the CSASS and put a round through his head, then switched targets. Before the mercenaries realized it, the second heavy gunner was down.

That got their attention. Four French fighters suddenly shifted their aim and laid down sustained fire on Cara's position. Chips of mud-brick and concrete sprayed over her. She flinched and dealt with another shooter, which brought even more bullets her way.

"Reaper, I don't know how much longer I can stay here," Cara told her team leader.

"Roger, Reaper Two. Pull back to the north. Do you remember the recon photos?"

"Copy."

"There was an old fountain area that looked like some kind of square, remember?"

"Affirmative."

"We'll pull back and meet you there."

"Copy that, out."

Kane said, "All callsigns listen up. We're getting out of here."

"How do you propose we do that?" Brick asked.

"Underground. We'll use the tunnel Brick found."

"How the fuck are we going to see down there?" Knocker asked. "Sorry, Reaper, but a man won't be able to see six inches in front of him down there."

"That means the French assholes won't be able to either," Kane pointed out.

"All right. If we're going, then we go now."

"OK, everyone down into the basement."

"I'll be right with you," Knocker replied. "I just

want to leave a little something for our friends."

"Don't be too long."

"You know me," the SAS man replied, and Kane imagined him smiling as he said it. "I'm always prompt and on time. Unlike some knobhead I won't mention."

"It was one time," Axe shot back over the comms.

"I didn't mention any names."

"Like I said, Knocker, don't be long, or you'll be finding your own way."

"I'll be right there."

———

The French mercenaries took a while to realize the gunfire from the battered building had ceased. Their commander waved two men forward to enter the structure and start sweeping it. He wasn't happy. He'd lost six men in the brief firefight. Worse, they were all killed. Three of his shooters had wanted to go after the sniper, but he'd halted them before they could do so. The shooting was sure to attract attention. If it wasn't militia, it would be Syrian troops or Russians.

His name was Pierre, and like most of his soldiers, he had served in the 1RPMIa *or1er Regiment Parachutiste D'Infanterie de Marine*, an arm of the French Special Forces. He turned to one of his men and said, "Get ready to move. I don't want to be here any longer than we need to be."

"What about the Americans?"

"They're gone. We need to find somewhere to lay up for the night and find them again tomorrow."

"Do you want me to call in the other team?"

Pierre was about to say no when an explosion erupted from the target building. He turned and watched the thick dust cloud filter from the building. The veins in his neck started to show as he snarled, *"Putain. Bâtards inutiles!"*

Now he was down to twelve men. "Get the rest into the vehicles. We're leaving."

———

Washington, DC

"There seems to be a problem," Brewer said. "Two, in fact."

Ares' blood ran cold. "What might those be?"

"The team in Maine lost the general," Brewer said. "And the Syria team had to pull out after Team Reaper gave them the slip."

Ares took a deep breath and let it out slowly. "Who was in charge in Maine?"

"Mister White."

"Uh-huh. What about the team in Syria?"

"They are French. We planned on using one of our own, but I thought it best to send one of the other teams into Syria just in case."

"Maybe you should have sent one of ours." Ares' voice was full of sarcasm.

"The French are good men," Brewer protested.

"If they're so good, why didn't they kill the bastards they were sent after?" Ares hissed.

"They will get them, I assure you."

"What about our Incirlik acquisition?"

"They are waiting to be transferred."

"I have an ask," Ares said.

"What would that be?"

"There is a friend of our cause who would like a certain person to be transferred to their custody. I said that it could happen, but not from a US airbase. I need you to see to it."

"I can do that."

"Good. I will send you the details."

"I'll be expecting them."

"Now, about the Syria team—"

"I already told you, they will handle it."

"Offer them all the assistance they need. No, I will reach out to Artemis myself and talk to him. Tell your people I'm displeased they have failed to find Hank Jones. Tell them I do not like failure."

The call ended abruptly, and Ares made the call to Artemis. "Ares, what can I do for you?"

"Your people failed to execute their mission properly, Artemis."

"Just a small setback, I assure you. They are very

good at what they do."

"I don't care how good they are. Just make sure Team Reaper does not make it out of Syria."

"I assure you—"

"I'm sick of people assuring me, Artemis. I fucking want results."

Once again, Ares ended the call abruptly and sat back, leaning into the soft leather of the chair.

There was a knock on the door, and Ares looked up. It swung open, and a young man in a suit entered. "I just thought you'd like to know that the marshals, FBI, Homeland, and all other law enforcement agencies are mobilizing to find General Jones."

"Thank you."

"And the vice-president should be sworn in within the next half an hour."

"Thank you."

The man exited and closed the door. Ares smiled. "So it begins."

CHAPTER 3

Aleppo, Syria

It took the team half an hour to stumble through the stygian darkness of the tunnel, but eventually, they found a way to the surface inside another semi-destroyed building almost two blocks to the east of where they'd started. By this time, the sun was low in the western sky, and they were pushed for time.

Before stepping out of their exit point, Kane sent Knocker ahead to recon their position. When he came back, he had news, not all of it good. "We've got militia between us and our objective, the fountain where you sent Cara. The good news is that we should be able to circle around them. It'll just take us longer, which means it'll be dark by the time we reach her."

Kane nodded. "Reaper Two, copy?"

There was no answer, so Kane tried again. "Reaper Two, this is Reaper One. Do you read me, over?"

"Copy, Reaper One."

"We're going to be a little longer than I figured. Find a hole and crawl into it, over."

"Roger that. Be aware, Reaper, that there are Syrian troops in the vicinity."

"Roger. See you soon. Out."

"Reaper Two, out."

Kane turned to Knocker. "Lead on, McDuff."

"As you wish, my lord."

With Knocker on point, they began making their way through the war-torn streets filled with rubble, discarded equipment, and burnt-out wrecks. Some buildings had been reduced to rubble, while others were just gone.

The SAS man kept the team to the darkened side of the streets, where the shadows were longest. Even though they saw no civilians, they could feel their gazes. Most had fled as refugees; however, there were those who had stayed, thinking they had nowhere else to go.

Then there were the remnants of the terror groups, ISIS and Al-Qaeda. Mostly they had been destroyed, but some of the militias were aligned with one or the other.

They reached an intersection and Knocker stopped them. "Wait up."

"What is it?"

"Looks like we got Syrian troops riding a roadblock at the intersection."

"This is the middle of enemy territory," Kane told him.

"Then they're some kind of militia who's taken uniforms off the dead."

"Find us a way around them, Knocker."

The SAS man crossed the street and started to lead the team around the roadblock. His 416 swept the way before him, never resting. Eventually, they made it past and continued to the rendezvous point.

"Reaper Two, copy?"

"Copy, Reaper One."

"Where are you?"

"I'm in the building on the northeast corner of the fountain."

Kane's gaze swept the plaza, looking for the building to which she had referred. "I've got you."

They gradually worked their way around the fountain, keeping to the shadows and trying to stay out of sight until they reached her.

"You finally made it, then," she greeted them.

"It took a while," Kane agreed. The sun was all but down.

They set up a perimeter, and Kane pulled Cara aside. "This is the Cabal."

She nodded. "Yes, and they're after all of us."

Kane nodded. "We need to get to Mersin and meet Slick. Regroup and go from there. Do you still have the satellite phone?"

"Yes. Why?"

"If there's one man who knows what the hell is going on, it's Hank Jones."

Cara passed it over, and Kane punched in a number he'd memorized a long time ago. A woman's voice on the other end said, "You've reached General Winkler's office."

Kane frowned. "I'm sorry, I think I've got the wrong number."

"Who were you looking for, sir?"

"General Hank Jones?"

There was a long pause before the woman said, "I'm sorry, sir, but General Jones isn't here anymore."

"I didn't know," Kane said, "I'm overseas."

"What is your name, sir? Maybe General Winkler can help you."

"Who's General Winkler?"

"He's the new chairman, sir. If I could just have your name—"

Kane disconnected. "Damn it."

"What is it?" Cara asked.

"Hank Jones isn't chairman anymore."

"What?" Cara's voice rose. She took a breath and asked, "Who is?"

"Someone named Winkler."

"Never heard of him, but you can bet he's got something to do with the Cabal."

"I need to find out what the hell is going on," Kane growled.

"How about you try the admiral?" Cara suggested.

Kane nodded. He punched in another number and waited. It rang, and a terse voice answered, "Joseph."

"Admiral, it's Kane."

Joseph's voice changed immediately. "Good Christ, man, where are you?"

"Aleppo. We're in a bit of a fix."

"You mean, you've been fucked over like everyone else."

"That sounds right. I need to know what's going on, Admiral. I tried General Jones, but he's been replaced."

Joseph sighed. "It's bad, son. They assassinated the President—"

"They *what*?"

"You heard me right. One of his detail faked a threat and shot him on the way to the bunker before shooting himself. The vice-president has been sworn in. They laid the assassination at the general's feet, and then they tried to kill him."

"Is he all right?"

"Scimitar and his boys are riding herd on him. They're headed—"

"Don't tell me, Admiral. Just as long as he's safe for now."

"What's going on, Reaper?"

"They sent a team of frogs after us in Aleppo. It was a setup. There was no HVT onsite."

"Shit. What about Mary?"

"All of Bravo except for Slick were taken into custody by CIA Director Brewer at Incirlik."

"Bastard."

"Sir, we're going dark. We'll extract ourselves from here and then see what we can do. I'll reach out when I can."

"Be careful, Reaper. This is bad. They've made their move, and I doubt it's going to stop anytime soon."

"I'll keep you in the loop as best I can, sir. Just don't believe all you hear."

"Good luck, Gunny."

"Thank you, sir."

Kane disconnected the call and powered the sat phone down to conserve the batteries. He looked at Cara and shook his head. "This is a whole lot worse than we first figured."

"What's happened?"

"Get everyone together. They all need to hear this."

A few minutes later, the team had gathered. "OK, listen up. The Cabal has made a big play—"

"We already knew that," Axe inserted.

Kane shook his head. "It's bigger than you think. The President has been assassinated—"

"Carter? Dead?" Brick asked in astonishment.

"That's not all. They've laid the blame at Hank Jones' feet. They sent a team after him, but Scimitar was able to extract him."

"This is a bloody cock-up," Knocker growled.

"It gets worse. They've put a new general in as Chairman. We have to believe he's Cabal. The vice president is now President."

"So we're pretty much fucked," Knocker growled again.

"We are if they get us. I told the admiral we're going dark. We need to get into Turkey to meet with Slick and plan our next move."

"First we have to get to Turkey," Brick said.

Kane nodded. "I'm up for ideas."

"Weelll—" Knocker started.

"Don't tell me you know someone out here," Cara commented.

"I might be able to find a bludger who's skiving off out here."

Cara reached for the satellite phone. "Work your magic, Sherlock."

"Wait," Kane snapped. "Do you trust whoever it is? The Cabal is worldwide, remember?"

"They're good blokes. I'd trust them with my life."

Kane nodded. "Do it."

A couple of minutes later, Knocker said to Kane as he handed the sat phone over, "They'll pick us up outside Aleppo about oh-nine-hundred."

"We'd better get moving then," he said. "It'll take us most of the night to get out of here."

Brick checked his magazine and replaced it, then spat on the ground and said, "Let's go. I'll take point."

Appalachian Mountains, Maine

The helicopter passed overhead for a second time, sweeping the ground in search of the fugitives. Inside the cave, the men waited for it to leave once again. As the rotor beat slowly faded, General Hank Jones said, "How long you figure they'll keep this up, Chief?"

Hunt stared at the darkness outside the cave mouth. "Depends, I guess. If they've got heat signature capabilities, the darkness is our enemy. We'll have to wait it out until morning to have a chance. If they don't, they'll give it up soon enough."

"I wish I knew what the hell was going on," Jones growled.

"They're trying to kill us, General," Hunt replied. "Be happy with that explanation."

"Sorry, Chief. I'm not a terribly good rabbit."

"Neither am I, General, but we've got to wait it out."

"We don't have to, Bord," Popeye said.

Hunt looked at him. "OK, Pop, I'm listening."

"How about we draw them in?"

"Keep going?"

"We light a fire and see what moths come to it. Set up our own ambush. Do a little shoot and scoot."

Hunt considered the proposal and how it could work before he said, "All right, we'll give it a try. There's still that helicopter to think of, though."

"It can't stay up here all night," Rucker said. "It's got to go refuel sometime."

"General, you get the veto."

"Screw that. Let's give those assholes something else to think about."

"Motion carried." Hunt grinned. "Let's do it."

———————

"The helicopter is reporting a fire one klick to our east," the man said to White.

"Tell them to investigate it and see if they can get any other heat signatures. We'll start moving in that direction."

"What if they scare them off?" the man asked.

"We need to keep them moving until morning," White told him. "Tired men make mistakes."

"I'll let them know."

———————

"Looks like the fire got someone's attention like we thought," Popeye said.

The volume of the helicopter's rotor grew as it drew closer. Suddenly it appeared above the trees, its landing lights strobing. Then a large spotlight under its belly came on and illuminated the fire area.

"They're looking to see if we're using the fire to mask our position," Hunt said above the rotor beat.

"How about we say hello, Chief?" Popeye asked.

"Shit, why not?"

The three shooters came out of the cave and opened fire on the low-hovering helicopter, their weapons on auto. A heavy stream of bullets streaked into the night sky. They could see flashes where the bullets struck the craft, and it suddenly veered to port.

The pilot must have worked the helicopter hard to get it out of the fire zone since it seemed to lurch away in the air. The motor coughed, and the aircraft suddenly fell from the sky. The illumination from the explosion lit the darkness, silhouetting the forest.

"Looks like we hit something that was essential to keeping that sucker in the sky," Rucker said.

"It does, don't it?" Hunt agreed. "Pop, get the general. We're leaving."

"What about waiting for them other assholes?"

"Nope, this is the window we need. Move."

———————

By dawn, they were still deep in the forest but some ten klicks from their last position. Popeye was on point, while Rucker was posted rear security. Hunt was riding shotgun on Hank Jones when the general said, "I need a break, Chief. I'm not ashamed to admit I'm not a young man anymore."

Hunt nodded. "It's OK, General. I am feeling it myself. You've come a lot farther than some men I know could."

"I'm trying, Chief."

Hunt said into his comms, "Hold up. Take five."

The four of them rested in situ, regaining their strength. Jones looked at Hunt and asked, "What are we doing, Bord?"

"E and E, General."

"I know that, damn it. But you've got a plan. I know you do."

Hunt nodded. "About twenty klicks southeast of here is a small holiday community. Once we reach it, I plan on stealing a vehicle and driving the rest of the way to Zulu Six."

"Scimitar! Danger close! Danger close!" Popeye's harsh, urgent whisper came through his comms. "I'm coming to you."

"Find a place to hide, General," Hunt said hurriedly. "We've got company."

They found cover in the thick undergrowth and waited. Popeye slid in beside them, but Rucker remained out on the perimeter. They waited, listening quietly for anything that might indicate the enemy's approach. When it happened, it was bizarre. The woods went quiet; one moment, there were birds chirping in the trees, then nothing.

Hunt found himself holding his breath, straining to hear the brush of material against a branch, the snap of a twig, the rustle of leaves. Then they appeared. Slowly at first, they seemed to materialize out of the dappled light. One, two, four...no, five. Five of them. A voice suddenly said, "Scimitar, you here?"

"Striker?" Hunt asked cautiously.

"It's me, buddy."

Hunt came to his feet and showed himself. "Over here."

The new arrivals walked forward. "Where's the rest of you?" Striker asked.

"What are you doing here, Striker?" the chief asked.

"The admiral sent us. Said to help escort a package to Zulu Six."

"Did he tell you anything else?"

Striker shook his head. "Just said there might be a few unfriendlies tagging along."

Hunt ran his gaze over the SEAL team. There were six of them. Striker was their leader, and Hunt knew him from past missions. But could they be trusted? He had to take that chance. He turned and said, "It's all right. Come on out."

The three men came to their feet, and Striker ran a cautious gaze over them that settled on General Hank Jones. "What the fuck is this, Scimitar?" he asked. "He killed the President."

"That's what they'd like you to believe, Striker. Truth is, they're trying to kill us."

"Really? Who's they?"

"The Cabal."

"The fucking *what*?"

Hunt was about to explain when the morning was ripped apart by gunfire.

———

"Get Barrel under cover!" Striker shouted at one of his men. He opened up with his M4A1 and sprayed the area the gunfire was coming from. Three of his men followed suit, while one worked to get his fallen comrade out of harm's way.

"Rucker, help that man," Hunt barked as he returned fire with his carbine.

The brush was alive with angry hornets, which, if touched, would deal a lot of damage. From his left, he heard Striker shout, "Jacks, Wire, flank those motherfuckers."

Hunt said into his comms, "Pop, keep an eye on the package."

"Roger that, Bord."

Then, "Striker, you on the channel?"

"Yeah. Who the fuck are these guys?"

"I already told you. We need to get out of here."

"We've got wheels about four klicks southeast of here."

"The general is the priority, Striker. He's the mission."

"Roger that. Let's get ready to travel."

"Rucker," Hunt continued as he fired at an unseen target. "What's the status of the casualty?"

"He took a round to his vest. He'll be fine."

"Get him ready to travel," Hunt ordered.

"Roger that."

The chief crawled through the brush to where Jones was sheltering behind a fallen tree trunk. "How you doing, General?"

"Just like back in Nam without the fucking air support, Chief," Jones growled.

"We're getting ready to move before they pin us down."

"Just tell me when."

"Striker, this is Scimitar, over."

"Read you Lima Charlie, Scimitar."

"Do you guys have some frag?"

"Roger that," Striker replied. "Where do you want it?"

"Wherever it's going to do us the most good."

"Keep your head down. Wire, Jacks, put some frag amongst those assholes and pull back to the last waypoint."

A few moments later, large explosions rocked the forest as the three fragmentation grenades detonated. Hunt looked at Jones and said, "Come on, General. On me."

It was far from a fighting retreat. It was more or less a rout, but the SEALs weren't too proud to do it. After all, they were outgunned in a hostile environment. The last thing they needed was for one of their own to go down or to lose the package.

They regrouped two kilometers from the site of the firefight. All seemed little the worse for wear except for Jones, who was blowing like a steam train pulling up a long, steep gradient. He gave Hunt a wry smile and said, "If this keeps up, I'll be running marathons next summer."

"Let's see that you make it, sir," Hunt said. He looked around for Striker. The tough-looking SEAL commander sensed he was being sought and glanced at him. "I'm thinking we should leave them something to think about on our back trail."

Striker nodded. "One of yours, one of mine?"

"Yeah."

"Roger that. Hammer, on me."

"Pop, over here."

Hunt said, "You two hang back and give them something to think about. Nothing too fancy; we don't want to lose you because you decided to be heroes. Got it?"

They nodded.

Striker said, "When you're done, we'll be working our way back along our route of insertion. I take it you still remember the trail, Hammer?"

The thin-faced operator smiled. "North of here,

wasn't it?"

"I'll give you fucking north. See you at the RV."

"Roger that."

Striker looked at Hunt. "Your package, so you're Bravo One."

"How about we put our heads together on that one?" Hunt suggested.

"Fine, I'm point. Don't get lost." He pressed the button on his comms. "Everyone move out."

CHAPTER 4

Aleppo, Syria

"Where the hell is your guy, Knocker?" Kane growled. "He was meant to have been here four hours ago at oh-nine-hundred."

"I have no idea, Reaper. I tried to contact him again, but he's off the grid."

"Maybe he was a dream," Axe offered.

"Fuck off, tosser."

"You want some?" Axe steamed.

"Better men than you have tried, Dobber. Bring it the fuck on."

Axe stepped forward and shoved the Brit in the chest. The instant reaction from the SAS man was a right fist that shot out and cracked Axe on the chin. Before it could go any further, Brick was between them, trying his best to keep them apart.

"Enough," Kane snapped. "That doesn't help."

Brick still had hold of the two men, and before he let them go, he asked, "We good?"

Knocker and Axe stared at each other in seething silence.

"I didn't hear you. *Are we good?*"

Axe nodded. "We're good."

"Knocker?"

The SAS man nodded too. "Yeah, we're good."

Brick let them both go. "What did you call him, anyway?"

"Dobber or tosser?"

"The second one."

"An idiot."

Brick laughed out loud, and it was followed by Axe. The big man said, "At least he didn't call me a dick."

With that, the tension was broken.

The team had been holed up in a rundown, shot-to-shit house at the edge of Aleppo. Their nine o'clock meeting hadn't eventuated. Kane had no intention of moving before dark anyway, so the best option was to hurry up and wait. Cara came over to him. "The natives are getting restless."

"Can you blame them?" he asked abruptly.

"Just saying is all," she replied. "Looks like they're not the only ones."

His gaze softened. "Sorry. I just feel—"

"Helpless? I think that's how we all feel."

"How are you doing?" Kane asked her.

"Like the rest of you, I expect."

Kane nodded. "Ammo check."

"Yeah, nothing like keeping busy. She pressed the talk button on her comms and said, "Everyone, ammo check."

Another hour elapsed before movement out on the desert drew Brick's attention. He raised a set of field glasses and saw four vehicles coming their way. He studied them for a moment, and a grin split his face. They were SAS Jackals. He pressed his talk button and said, "Reaper One. Tell Knocker his friends have arrived."

Five minutes later, the four Jackals pulled up.

"I was told you lot needed a ride," the warrant officer said.

"Where the hell have you been, Knobby?" Knocker growled. "Not good for a lad's reputation when you show up this bloody late."

"Had a brief discussion with some Syrian troops. Anyway, we're here now. What's going on?"

Knocker introduced Kane, and the Team Reaper commander told him what they already knew. The SAS man frowned. "And you lot want to go into the lion's den once more?"

"That's it. We need to get to our people and work out what to do from there."

"I wish you luck, Sergeant. We'll get you to Turkey. From there, I'm not sure there's any more we can do."

"That'll be enough," Kane said.

"All right, climb aboard."

Ankara, Turkey

They were placed in three cells, hot, fetid, sandstone boxes that would be cramped for one, let alone two or three. The women were together in one cell, Ferrero and Teller were in another, and Traynor and Arenas were in the last. This was their second day in captivity in the military prison. They were informed that they would be tried for the airstrike within the week, and after that, they would face execution. Being found guilty was only a formality.

Footsteps sounded along the cobblestone hallway and stopped outside the iron door where Thurston, Reynolds, and Morales were being held. The key rattled in the lock, then the door screeched open on dry hinges.

Two armed men appeared in the doorway. One was a lieutenant named Demir, but the other the women hadn't seen before. Demir pointed at Thurston. "The general wants to see you."

Thurston didn't move. "Do I get to shower first? I'm pretty ripe."

"You come now."

She shrugged. "OK then, but don't say I didn't

warn you."

The second man stepped forward and held out chains. He put them on Thurston's wrists and ankles before guiding her through the open door. As she left the cell area, she called, "Don't wait up."

The hallway led to a large dining room, and then she was taken to the commandant's office, a general named Kadir. Upon reaching the office, the general was surprised to see that Brewer was there, along with another dark-haired man standing looking out a window with his back to her.

Thurston stared hard at Kadir and asked, "You know what you're doing will have dire repercussions, right?"

Kadir shrugged. "Who will know? Who will care? You and your team went rogue and killed innocent civilians. I could execute you on live television and nothing would happen."

"We did no such fucking thing," Thurston seethed.

"We have it all on record," Kadir told her. "Your CIA provided all that we need."

"Yeah, well, he's a fucking lying asshole too."

Brewer smiled coldly. "I told you, General, she will try everything to get herself out of this."

"At least she will not be my problem any longer. It is a pity she can't be executed along with the rest of them."

"It was part of the deal, General, remember?"

Kadir sighed. "Yes, you don't need to remind me."

Hearing those words concerned Thurston more than staying to be executed. At least they were all together here, and there was a slight chance they could do something about getting out. But if they were being separated, then… "Where am I going?"

The man turned away from the window, and for the first time, Thurston saw his face. Her eyes widened and her face blanched when she recognized who he was. A mirthless smile split the man's thin lips. "Why, with me, of course."

———————

"Where do you figure they've taken her?" Teller asked.

"Who knows?"

"She's been gone a long time," he said.

Ferrero nodded. "Too long."

He didn't want to think about it. The general could be being tortured, questioned, or… The last possibility didn't bear thinking about.

"Luis, you there?"

It was Traynor. "Yeah."

"We need a plan."

"I know. I already have one."

"What's that?"

"Wait for Reaper."

"You figure he's coming?"

"He'll come. As long as he's still breathing, he'll come."

———————

Mersin, Turkey

It took them two days to reach Mersin, Turkey. The SAS team got them back across the border and supplied them with a couple of old Land Rovers. They hid all their gear in the back of the vehicles, except for the handguns they kept on their person. Their biggest problem was going to be that if they got pulled over, none of them had any ID. When they finally reached Mersin, Kane reached out to Slick.

"We're here."

"Find somewhere to lay up, Reaper, and I'll come to you," he said. "Give me a call when you do, and then I'll come. That way I can pinpoint your location."

"You have any trouble?"

"No."

"Give me ten minutes to find somewhere."

"Roger that," Slick said and disconnected.

After ten minutes, he turned on the sat phone again and called Swift. "We've found a position."

A few seconds later, Swift said, "I like it. I'll be with you directly."

The line went dead and Kane looked at Cara,

who was behind the wheel of the Land Rover. "He's coming."

"How much illegal shit do you think is in these containers?" she asked.

The place they had chosen to lay up was a large railyard full of shipping containers. Across the road from their position was another yard full of containers, and beyond that was the port of Mersin. Kane shrugged. "A lot, in all probability."

The team waited for thirty minutes before Swift showed. He appeared around the corner of a container farther down the yard, and Axe saw him approach. "The computer geek is here," he said over his comms.

When Kane laid eyes on him, the man looked tired. "How you doing, Slick?"

"Man, is it good to see you guys. I've been living on nerves and jumping at shadows ever since the thing went down at Incirlik."

"Do you know where they were taken?" Kane asked, meaning the rest of Bravo team.

Swift shook his head. "No. They were hit with some bullshit charge, though."

"What charge?"

"They were blamed for a drone attack in Ankara. Civilians were killed."

"When did it happen?"

"It didn't. Not a UAV attack, anyway. It was a car bomb."

"How do you know that?" Cara asked.

"I've studied these things long enough to know. Besides, I did some digging around in electronic back rooms, and there was no UAV over Turkey at that time."

"So, it's a setup," Knocker said. "With the Turkish judicial system the way it is, they're as good as executed."

Kane's face grew grim. "We need a location for the rest of the team, and we have to find out what went on with that bomb."

"To find out where the team was taken means a trip to Incirlik," Cara pointed out. "I'll go."

"I'll go with you," Brick added.

Swift said, "You'll need a way onto the base. I can do that."

"That'll work," Kane agreed. "I'll take Axe and Knocker with me, and we'll have a look at the bombing site. We might be able to find something."

"What about me?" asked Swift.

"Somebody planted that bomb. I need you to sift through every bit of camera footage, satellite feed, and whatever else you can link into to see if you can get a lead on them."

"That's easy. It'll be the CIA."

"Find them, Slick."

He nodded. "Roger that."

"Heads up, we've got incoming," Brick said over his comms. "And they don't look friendly."

"Break out the weapons," Kane ordered. "Let's give them a good old-fashioned welcome."

There were four vehicles in all: four vehicles, twelve shooters. The French were back. "Are they who I think they are?" Cara asked as she watched them through her sights on the CSASS.

"Looks to be," Kane agreed.

"How the hell did they find us here?"

"Ask me an easier question."

"I think I know," Swift said.

They looked at him.

"They might have traced back to my computer when I…" He shrugged.

"Damn it, Slick! I thought you were more careful than that."

"It's been a hell of a last few days."

"It's about to get worse. Reaper One to all call-signs. Wait for my command."

The French mercenaries separated into teams of two and filtered into the city of shipping containers. Their movements were tracked by unseen suppressed weapons.

"Reaper, now would be a good time to send those guys a message," Axe muttered into his comms.

"Wait for it."

Kane allowed the mercenaries to infiltrate farther into the stacks of containers. From beside him, Cara said, "I can't get a decent shot amongst this shit, Reaper. I'm ineffective as a sniper. Luckily, I came prepared."

Kane looked at her and saw that she'd removed the scope. She grinned at him, "Now I'm ready."

"Reaper One to all callsigns. Let's go hunting."

The first fusillade of weapons fire saw four mercenaries fall. After that, things got a little crazy.

On the left side of the yard, Knocker pushed forward to a position where he was able to observe a couple of Frenchmen disappearing behind a container stack. He reached the corner and cautiously peered around. Immediately the rattle of gunfire sounded, and howling ricochets from the steel side of the twenty-foot box scythed through the air.

The Brit leaned out and fired a short burst at the two shooters, but he missed. He ducked back as more bullets clattered into the side of the container. If he stayed there, he'd get pinned down.

Knocker decided to circle around the other way and see if he could get behind them, so he began backing up. That was obviously what the mercenaries had decided to do because when he moved around the corner of the container, he walked into a single Frenchman sneaking up on him.

The SAS man's movements were all reflex, muscle memory. He dropped the 416 and let it hang by its strap while his left hand grabbed the barrel of the mercenary's weapon. Knocker's right hand drove downward and came back up filled with his M17. He drove the barrel into the chest armor of the Frenchman and fired four times.

The force of the blows was telling as the mercenary staggered and then dropped to his knees. None of the shots were lethal, but the next one was. Knocker placed the M17 a couple of inches from the man's forehead and shot him, dropping him to the ground like a rag doll. He didn't move again.

Knocker replaced the handgun in its holster and retrieved the 416, then moved swiftly around the container until he cornered the second mercenary. His carbine fired, and the Frenchman fell. Knocker took a deep breath and moved on to find another target.

Brick edged into a narrow opening between two containers as he tried to flank another pair of mercenaries attempting to do the same to Axe. As he slid between the ridged freight boxes, he said into his comms, "Axe, you've got two Frenchies trying to flank you on your left. Watch your fire. I'm working to come up behind them."

"Copy."

Brick suddenly felt a cold hand grip his heart as he realized he'd fucked up. The two mercenaries had drawn him into a perfect kill zone. He looked up and saw two grinning figures looking down at him, their FAMAS F1 assault rifles ready to fire.

"Stupid ass," Brick admonished himself.

The former SEAL braced himself for what was about to happen, but when the sound of gunfire reached his ears, it wasn't the cracks he was expecting. It was the flattened reports of suppressed fire.

The two shooters fell like stones from the containers to the hard-packed earth between the boxes. Brick looked up and found Axe with a big shit-eating grin on his unshaven face, the SAW in his hands. "Getting old, Brickster."

"Fuck off."

"You're welcome."

Kane and Cara worked as a team, him bringing down two shooters while she picked off another one. That left one. The team began working him like a dog with a herd of cattle. When they finally had him cornered, he was given the opportunity to surrender.

"You've got no hope, my friend," Kane declared loudly. "We give you this one chance. Tell us who sent you, and we'll let you walk away."

"They said you were good at what you do," the Frenchman explained. "Maybe I should have brought more men."

"What's your name?"

"Pierre."

"You want to drop your weapons, Pierre?"

The Frenchman dropped his carbine in the dirt but retained his sidearm. Kane asked, "Who sent you, Pierre?"

The man was silent for a moment, then shrugged resignedly. "I'm dead anyway. I was sent by Artemis."

"Who's Artemis?"

"He is the French version of your Ares."

Kane snapped a glance at Cara before asking, "What's his name?"

Pierre shook his head. "I do not know."

"Are you sure?"

"All I know is that he works for our French government."

Kane glanced at Swift. "How many French names were on that list we found?"

"I'll have to look it over. There were some, but I should be able to narrow it down."

"Do it later. Right now, we need to get going before the authorities show up." Reaper looked at Pierre. "You can join us if you want."

The Frenchman was surprised by the offer but shook his head. "I have failed in my mission and must now pay the price for that failure."

"You're really going to do that?" Kane asked.

The Frenchman nodded. "It is the only way."

Without warning, Kane drew his M17 and shot Pierre twice, dropping him where he stood. He turned to the others and said, "Back to the vehicles. We need to get out of here."

CHAPTER 5

Somewhere over the Atlantic

The Bombardier Global 6000 flew at a cruising altitude of forty-one thousand feet over the choppy white water of the Atlantic. It was on its return leg to Washington, DC from Turkey, and Brewer was relaxing with a glass of bourbon. That good mood, however, was about to be shattered by an incoming phone call.

"Brewer."

"It would seem that the Reaper Team was more resourceful and resilient than we factored in," the voice on the other end said in a heavy French accent.

"What happened?"

"The mercenaries are all dead. They were killed in Mersin, Turkey."

Brewer sat forward. "Turkey? How on earth did they reach Turkey?"

"I don't know, but they must have had help. Do you want me to send another team?"

"No, I will take care of it."

"As you wish."

The line went dead, and Brewer began punching numbers for an urgent call to Turkey.

The recipient of that call was Kadir, who picked up on the second ring. Without speaking, he heard, "I need you to assemble a team. The people who were meant to die in Syria are on Turkish soil."

"Why is this my problem?"

"Because these are resourceful people. If you don't stop them, they will eventually find out where their people are and come for them."

"This will cost more money."

Brewer sighed. "I'm aware of that. Just see to it."

The call disconnected, and Brewer made yet another call. This one, he wasn't looking forward to.

"I hope you have good news for me?" Ares asked.

"I wouldn't exactly call it good news."

"Really?" The question was cloaked in sarcasm.

"The French team was killed in Turkey."

His words were met with stony silence.

"I have had General Kadir put together a team to look for them," Brewer explained.

"But?"

"He wants more money."

"What did you tell him?"

"Nothing."

"I'll have it organized," Ares said with a hint of dissatisfaction. "What is happening with the team hunting Hank Jones?"

He'd almost forgotten about that. "They are still on the run. It seems they got some assistance from another SEAL team."

"Joseph?"

"Most probably."

"I was hoping he wouldn't be a problem," Ares said. "When you get back, keep an eye on him. If we need to, we can find a dark hole to keep him in until we are done."

"Wouldn't it be simpler to kill him?"

"I think a President and a chairman will suffice for the moment."

"Speaking of Presidents, how is the new one doing?"

"He is looking over a proposal to send troops to Ukraine."

"Progress already," Brewer said. "You work fast."

"That is why I'm Ares. I'll see you when you return."

Brewer stared at the phone in his hand as the screen darkened. The right choice had indeed been made.

———————

Zulu Six, Allegheny Mountains

"It's good to hear you're all right, Hank," Joseph said to his friend. "I was afraid you might not make it."

Jones looked around at the old buildings surrounded by peaks and dense forest. "Would have been if not for you sending me more of your boys, Alex."

"It was the least I could do after those fuckers set you up the way they did."

"How is it in Washington, Alex?"

"They've sworn Nelson into office. Thomas Winkler is in your seat."

"Never liked that asshole. Now I know why," Jones remarked.

"He's advocating to send troops to Ukraine. Shit, the President has only been in office for a minute, and they're trying to play him like a fiddle."

"Tell me this: why did they kill Carter? For an entity living in the shadows, they certainly came out in a big way."

"My guess is that it was because of the attention. He'd become a liability," Joseph theorized.

"But we know that from the list there's more than one country involved in this Cabal," Jones pointed out.

"America is the bigger partner, I guess."

"Which means that they took a big risk getting rid of Carter."

"Unless they already had someone to replace him," Joseph countered.

"But who? Nelson?"

Joseph snorted derisively. "Come on, Hank. You know a dull spark is brighter than that asshole. No, he's there because he can be manipulated."

"If that's true, it has to be someone close."

"Leave it with me, Hank. I'll see what I can work out."

"Be careful, Alex. These people play for keeps," Jones warned. Then, "Maybe there's another way. How about we go after someone on the list? High up."

"You have someone in mind?"

"What about Solomon Harris?"

"Maybe."

"You know where he is?"

"I'll find out," Joseph said. "Then I'll get back to you."

"Thanks, Alex."

"Stay safe, Hank."

———

Mersin, Turkey

The team found a place to lay up for the night, which seemed quiet enough, but they still maintained a rotating watch. Slick was working on a way to get Cara and Brick into the base at Incirlik before he began searching for something that would some-how prove the innocence of Bravo element. It was three in the morning when he found what he was looking for. He shook Kane awake. "Reaper, I've got something."

"I'll be right there," the team leader replied, still half-asleep.

Swift went back to his computer, and when Kane joined him, he had Cara with him. "What do you have, Slick?"

They moved behind him as he unfroze the video on the screen before them. "Have a look at this."

The footage showed a man parking a Renault and exiting the vehicle. He walked away and didn't return.

"Are you able to get a look at his face?" Kane asked.

"Yes, and I ran it as best I could without setting off any alarms. Came up with nothing."

"How about tracking his movements?"

"I'm working on that, but let's jump forward with this, shall we?"

Swift ran the feed forward. It darkened and then lightened once more. Kane nodded. "Ballsy. They left it there overnight so as not to raise suspicions."

About three hours after dawn, the car exploded in a flash and the feed ceased. "So, that's our bomb," Cara said. "How did they come up with a rogue UAV story?"

"Two things," Swift said. "I'm guessing that was the line fed to them by the CIA—"

"But they'd still need proof," Kane interrupted.

Swift hit a button and the picture changed. It showed pieces of metal lying in the street, only there was something much smaller lying amongst them. Cara leaned forward. "Can you zoom in and blow that up?"

Swift did as he was asked.

"Is that a fin?" Cara asked.

"That's what all the reports are saying."

"There's no way it would be that straight after a blast. No chance in hell."

"Find out where that guy went after he left the Renault. I want to ask him some questions."

"I'm on it."

———————

The sun was just coming up when he found the location of the man in question. Once more he woke Kane. "I found him."

This time Kane got everyone up. They gathered around, and Swift began to fill them in. "Our guy lives here."

The picture he had was from a satellite. It showed a house with a large yard and a pool. "Just like the CIA to have all the good things," Axe growled.

"Is all this secure?" Brick asked. "Remember what happened the last time."

"It's as secure as I can make it. Now, as for the

house. I've counted at least five people there. I'd say it's a little more than your average safehouse. More like a CIA base of operations for the region."

"Good work, Slick."

"They aren't going to give up their friend willingly, Reaper," Brick said.

"Then we take him," Knocker suggested.

"There might be innocents in there, Reaper. Might be there is only one bad apple."

"I guess we'll find out," Kane said. "Now, what about Incirlik?"

"Cara and Brick shouldn't have any problems getting in. Getting out could be an issue."

"Why?"

"Well, you're walking onto a part-American airbase to interrogate the commander, so…" He left it unfinished.

"It's the only way to find out what happened to the others," Kane pointed out.

"This is your lucky day, Reaper. I did some digging, and once a week, our friendly neighborhood commanding officer goes off-base to meet with a certain lady."

"I take it the certain lady is not his wife?" Cara asked.

"Bingo! Right on the money."

Cara glanced at Kane. "It would be easier that way."

"All right, work it out with Brick."

"Roger that."

Kane looked at his people. "We leave in an hour. Get ready."

"Reaper," Swift said. "I think I would be better—"

"You're coming with us," Kane said, cutting him off.

"Really?" There was an edge of eagerness in his voice.

"Yes, in case we need you to hack into the CIA database."

"Fantastic."

"Don't get too excited."

"Too late."

Zulu Six, Allegheny Mountains

"I need you to do a job for me, Chief," Jones said to Hunt. "You'll need a small team to carry it out."

It was 10pm, and Joseph had just called to inform Jones of his target's location.

Hunt nodded. "All right."

"It's a snatch-and-grab."

"Who's the target?" he asked.

"Solomon Harris."

Hunt looked at Striker, then back to Jones. "I don't mean to question the decision, General, but why?"

"We need to get a line on who Ares is," Jones explained. "We know Harris is on the list, so the only way to find out is to pick him up."

"We don't even know where…" He knew Jones wouldn't be suggesting the mission if he didn't know where the mining magnate was. "Where is he, sir?"

"New York."

"That's twelve up and twelve back, give or take a few," Hunt pointed out.

"I know, Chief."

"Not to mention, he could have bodyguards."

Jones nodded. "You should probably count on it."

"I'll take Rucker and—"

"I'll go with Scimitar," Striker interrupted, volunteering.

Hunt looked at him and then nodded. "All right. Three should do. If we leave now, we can do most of our traveling tonight."

"If you need anything, reach out to Alex."

"Yes, sir."

"Don't forget, we need him alive."

"He'll be alive, General," Hunt said. "I can't say what kind of shape he'll be in, though."

"Just as long as he can talk, Chief. Just as long as he can talk."

———————

Washington, DC

"Where are you?" Brewer asked.

"Langley," White replied.

"What the hell are you doing there?" the CIA director growled into his cell.

"Trying to pick up a trail."

"You still haven't found him?"

"No."

"Christ. Wait for me there."

Brewer disconnected and growled to his driver, "Take me to Langley."

"Yes, sir."

Langley, Virginia

The operations room was small. Smaller than the main one they used, anyway. This one was for "special" missions, the deep, dark kind that hid under rocks you didn't want to be disturbed. It took a different type of person to work in the room, and each of these people was different.

"What do you have?" Brewer asked White when he entered.

White said, "I think we have a lead, maybe even a location."

The CIA director nodded. "Go on."

"We've been using satellite imagery, plus a whole heap of other stuff I won't bore you with to try and get a fix. After coming up on a dead-end a couple of times, I think..." he nodded at the screen, "this might be where they're holed up."

"What is it?"

"It's an old SEAL training base far away from anything they use today," White informed him. He looked at one of the console operators. Bring it up on heat."

The screen changed, and Brewer saw what White was getting at. "Where is this?"

"In the Alleghenies. A place called Zulu Six."

"Take a team up there. Get me results."

New York

"Where do you figure he's going?" Striker asked as they tailed the Chevy Tahoe.

Light from street lamps flickered across their faces as they drove along the narrow thoroughfare. Ahead of them riding passenger was Solomon Harris. Traveling with him, apart from the driver, was a bodyguard. It was obvious from his bearing that he was ex-military of some type.

Hunt looked at his watch. "This time of the day, I expect not home."

Keeping up their tail at a discreet distance, when the Tahoe entered a parking garage in Manhattan, they followed it into the garage and pulled into a vacant space twenty meters away. They watched as Harris got out and was escorted to the elevator. "Wonder what this place is?" Rucker asked.

"Don't matter much. This is where we take him."

"I'll take care of the driver," Striker volunteered.

He climbed out of the vehicle and made his way casually over to the Tahoe. Hunt watched as he bent down to pick up something from the concrete floor, then knock on the window as though to ask whether they had dropped a fifty. When the man buzzed the window down, the SEAL commander smashed the driver's face with one blow without warning, and after a quick scuffle, Striker opened the door and pulled the driver clear.

He hid the driver behind the vehicle and signaled to the others. Hunt said, "Stay here and be ready."

"Yes, sir."

Hunt got out and hurried across to the Tahoe. "You kill him?"

Striker shook his head. "No. I just hope he don't wake up in a hurry."

"See if you can find something in the SUV to restrain him if he does."

The SEAL did as instructed, finding handcuffs, duct tape, and some lengths of rope. He held them up and said, "What the fuck is this guy into?"

"I'll ask him if you want?" Hunt said. "Maybe he can show you if we have time."

"I'll pass, thanks."

With the driver secure, they settled down to

wait. Hunt took the driver's hat and coat and stood waiting with his back to the way Harris and his bodyguard would approach.

An hour later, they appeared. Hunt let them come to him, not even bothering to acknowledge they were there.

"Mike?" Harris called when they'd almost reached the Tahoe.

Hunt remained still.

Harris tried again. "Mike?"

Hunt turned and stared directly at the mining magnate. Harris' eyes widened as realization set in. His bodyguard moved for his weapon, but Striker was on him, giving him no chance to get the weapon clear. The barrel of the SEAL's handgun pressed hard against the base of the bodyguard's skull. Striker said, "If you think you're having a bad day now, sport, just pull that thing."

The bodyguard froze.

"Good choice," Striker said and hit him hard enough to knock him cold, letting him slump to the concrete floor.

"Who are you?" The words spoken by Harris held an element of uncertainty as well as a demand.

"We're going to take you for a ride, asshole," Hunt said. "There's someone who wants to ask you some questions."

"I'm going no—"

Hunt hit him, not hard enough to knock him

down, but enough to make him bleed and take notice. "You shut the fuck up and do as we say."

There was a roar of an engine, and Rucker pulled their vehicle close. They bundled Harris into it and drove off.

———————

Zulu Six, Allegheny Mountains

As Popeye stood on the veranda of one of the rundown buildings at Zulu Six, he felt the hairs on the back of his neck stand erect. Gripping the H&K417 tighter, he scanned the surroundings, looking for any indication that they weren't alone. Then slowly and deliberately, he said into his comms, "All callsigns check in."

"Hammer all clear."

"Anvil all clear."

"Jacks all clear."

Then there was silence. A cold tingling ran down Popeye's spine. "Barrel and Wire, check in."

Nothing.

"Barrel and Wire, check in."

Nothing.

"Barrel—"

The day suddenly lit up with gunfire. The valley in which Zulu Six was nestled was rocked by the staccato sound. Popeye dove off the veranda onto the ground behind a large concrete block. His comms lit up as the others started calling in.

"Hammer taking fire!"

"Anvil taking fire. Pinned down."

"Jacks under heavy fire, two o'clock."

"Everyone, fall back," Popeye ordered.

Popeye brought up his 417 and used the scope to search for targets. They were all in the tree line, which made them hard to pick out. One shooter was hunkered behind a fallen pine with only a minimal portion of himself visible, but for a practiced sniper like the SEAL, it was sufficient. Popeye squeezed the trigger, and the designated marksman's weapon slammed back into his shoulder.

The shooter fell back and never reappeared.

"Damn it, check in," Popeye growled.

"Coming in, Pop," Anvil called as he broke cover. Bullets chased him as he ran toward Popeye's position. He skidded to a halt and dropped beside him. "This is fucked."

"Man down!" That call was the one Popeye had been dreading. "Hammer is—"

The transmission stopped abruptly. Popeye pressed his talk button. "Hammer, come in."

Silence.

"Hammer, copy?"

The SEAL was gone.

"Jacks, where are you?"

"I'm coming to you. Three o'clock."

Popeye moved his 417 and looked through his

scope. He could see the operator bounding down a rocky slope between the trees.

"How the fuck did this happen?" Anvil growled.

"Worry about that later. Get inside and get the general."

"And do what, Pop?"

Popeye told him, and Anvil looked at him questioningly. "You sure about this?"

"Yes, so go."

Anvil came to his feet amid a storm of bullets. Keeping his head low, he ran up the steps onto the veranda and hit the door with his shoulder. It flew back, and he lunged inside as rounds punched into the doorjamb.

"Jacks, how far away are you?"

"I'm circling around. I'll be there in a couple of mikes."

"Forget it. Meet Anvil at building three."

"Copy. Building three."

With that done, Popeye did a tactical reload and began looking for more targets. It was time to earn his pay.

———

When Anvil burst through the door, Jones almost shot him with the weapon Hunt had loaned him. He realized who it was and asked, "What's going on, son?"

"I'm here to get you out, sir."

"Where are we going?"

"Wherever they aren't."

"How the hell are we meant to get there?" Jones snapped. "Besides, I need to get to Washington to sort this shit out."

"Call it a tactical regroup, sir. Besides, this ain't a debate. You're going one way or the other."

Jones stared at the sandy-headed SEAL and nodded. "All right. What about the others?"

"They'll join us if they can."

"What do you mean?"

"I don't have time for this shit, sir. Out the back. Move."

Anvil began guiding him out the rear. "Go that way," he ordered, pointing at another rundown building. On the other side of the structure they'd just left, gunfire echoed noisily. They crossed the gravel path to the next building, and Jacks appeared. He had a cut on his cheek and more blood on his left sleeve. "You OK, brother?"

"I'll live. The others?"

"I guess we're it."

"What about Pop?"

Anvil shook his head.

"Fuck." Jacks pressed his comms button. "You with me, Pop?"

"Get the fuck out of here," the voice came back. It didn't sound right, and Jacks looked at Anvil.

"Come on, Jacks, let's go."

"We can't just fucking leave him."

"Get your head in the game, Jacks."

"Fuck you, I ain't leaving. You go. Me and Pop will find you."

Anvil shook his head.

"Go, Matt," Jacks said, this time mellower.

"All right. But remember, the general is the mission."

"Always was."

Anvil watched him leave, then turned to Jones. "I hope what we're doing is fucking worth it."

"So do I, son, so do I."

Jacks came down the steps and parked himself beside Popeye, who was as pale as a ghost but still in the fight. Then he saw that the SEAL was crouched in his own blood. "Damn it, Pop, are you all right?"

"What are you doing back here, Jacks?" Popeye growled.

"Wasn't going to leave you."

A bullet ricocheted off the concrete block. Popeye fired off the rest of his magazine and flopped down, working with blood-slick fingers to change it out. "Fucking round got under my armor. One in a million shot, you know that?"

He dropped the magazine as he tried to reload. "Shit."

Jacks snatched the 417 from him. "Give me that."

Reloading the weapon, he went to pass it back when the crack of a bullet made him duck. "That was close."

He turned to look at Popeye, who was not taking the weapon, and saw the SEAL staring blankly at him, the light of life gone from his eyes. "Damn it, Pop! What did you have to go and die for?"

Jacks left his M4A1 on its strap and started using the 417, looking around for targets. He found one and put him down before a storm of bullets peppered his position and he had to wait for a break. When it came, he rose and saw three men emerge from the trees. He sighted and fired, shifted his aim, and repeated the action.

Both shots dropped their respective targets. The SEAL shifted aim again and sighted on the remaining shooter. His finger tightened on the trigger, but the shot never came.

When the bullet hit, it hit hard. The air left Jacks' lungs with a whoosh, and his jaw dropped. He tried desperately to draw in a breath, but it was hard.

Jacks reached down and felt the wetness of the wound. As he slumped down next to his dead companion, he cursed under his breath. Pain was starting to radiate out from the wound. He reached up and pressed his transmit button on his comms. "Anvil, buddy?"

"Yeah, I got you, Jacks."

"You'll have to go downrange on your own this

time, *amigo.*"

"What's going on, Jacks?" Anvil's voice held more than a hint of urgency.

"They…" He swallowed as he felt the blood well up in his throat. "They got me good this time."

"Hang on, Jacks. I'll come—"

"No!" he hissed into his comms. "Remember, the general is the mission. Keep him alive until Scimitar and Striker can get to you."

"I'm sorry, Jacks."

"Roger that. Now fuck off."

Jacks slumped against the concrete block next to Popeye. He gasped for air, looked at the vast blue sky above him, and wondered why he had never spent time looking at the beautiful depth of color it could take on. "It's been a hell of a life," he muttered to himself.

A shadow fell across him and Jacks blinked, trying to focus on the face of the man standing over him. He blinked again, and it swam into view. The man smiled at him and said, "I guess you're about all done in, huh? There is something, though, before you cash in your chips. How about you tell me where the general is?"

Jacks chuckled and spat blood at White. "Fuck you, asshole."

White shook his head. "It doesn't matter. We'll find him. Then you'll have died for nothing."

White raised his handgun and shot Jacks in the head.

CHAPTER 6

Adana, Turkey

Cara and Brick watched Colonel Grady Brooks pull into the driveway of a house seemingly constructed from a variety of different-sized boxes just slapped together. However, it was nice and spoke of money.

"I bet you fifty she's married," Brick offered.

"I'm not going to take that bet," Cara replied.

From inside the vehicle, they heard a dog bark somewhere down the street. The darkness was faintly illuminated by a crescent moon, and the cloudless sky meant the air had a sharp chill to it. The other houses on the street had lights on, which meant that when they moved, they had to be careful. Any indication of trouble and they'd have Turkish authorities coming down on them like a blizzard. They'd likely not see the light of day for years.

"You want the back or front?" Brick asked.

"I'll take the front. If the woman answers, she won't be as on edge as if it were a man."

"How are you going to get past her?"

"I'll think of something."

Brick checked his M17. "You know we look out of place in our BDUs, right?"

"Can't do much about that," Cara replied. She glanced at her watch; it was 21:00 local time. "Let's go."

They slipped out of their Land Rover and closed the doors. Using the shadows as much as they could until they reached the house, Cara gave Brick time enough to slip around to the rear of the building. When he said, "In position" over the comms, she went up to the front door and knocked. Not tentatively, but like a person with authority.

Cara took half a step back and placed her right hand behind her back, the SIG firmly grasped in it. A few moments later, a pretty, long-haired woman who was somewhere in her late thirties answered. What surprised Cara the most was that the woman was obviously not Turkish.

"Can I help you, soldier?" she asked. "Are you here for my husband?"

Holy shit!

"Yes, ma'am."

"I'll just get him for you."

"Thank you, ma'am."

As soon as she disappeared, Cara said into her comms, "Brick, it's his fucking wife."

"Why weren't we told?"

"I don't know."

"Shit."

"He's coming to the front door. Get your ass around here. Now."

Brick started running back around from the rear of the house. By the time he got around to the front, Cara had her weapon jammed under his chin. "Back the hell up, motherfucker. We've got things to talk about."

"What the hell is this?" Brooks gasped.

"Not here."

Cara forced him back, and Brick closed the door. "Now, asshole, turn around and take us into the living room."

They followed him into the living room, where his wife was waiting. She stared at them wide-eyed. "Grady, what's going on?"

"Are there any kids in the house?" Cara snapped.

"What?"

"Are there any children in the house?"

"N-no."

She glanced at Brick. "Have a look."

The big ex-SEAL nodded and started to search the house. Cara looked at Brooks. "This woman's your wife?"

"Ex."

"Explains why she's living off-base, I guess. Why didn't you go back to the US?"

"We're trying…" She paused. "Why the fuck am I telling you this shit?"

Cara said, "You just sit there nice and quiet, and this'll be over right quick."

Her eyes went back to Brooks. "What do you want?" he asked.

"Are you part of them or just a pawn?" Cara demanded.

"What?"

"The Cabal, Colonel."

His face paled.

Brick reappeared. "There's no one else here."

"I told you," Brooks' ex-wife spat.

"What's your name?" Cara asked.

"Laura."

"Well, Laura, how about you let us get on with what we came here for?"

"Just kill us and get on with it," Laura snarled.

Cara smiled. "I like you. Military?"

She nodded.

"We aren't here to kill you. Your husband, on the other hand? That really depends on what he tells us."

"I don't know anything."

"Jog his memory, Brick."

Brick took a few steps forward and hit Brooks a solid blow to his face. Not enough to knock him senseless, but enough to remind him who was in charge.

"Stop!" Laura cried.

"Looks like someone still loves you, Grady," Cara observed. "Wonder if she will after she finds out how you betrayed our people?"

"What's she talking about, Grady?"

"I don't know," he hissed.

"Come on, Colonel. Let me jog your memory a little more. What about CIA Director Paul Brewer?"

"I don't know."

Brick hit him again, this time without an invitation from Cara. More blood flowed.

Shaking her head, Cara said, "Are they that scary, Colonel?"

He glared at her defiantly.

"Damn it, someone tell me what is going on?" Laura almost screamed.

Cara raised her eyebrows as Brooks remained silent. "No? Looks like it has to be me. Let's start with being left behind in Syria."

"What?" Laura blurted.

"Our team was on an op in Syria after an HVT that never existed. In fact, there were a bunch of French mercenaries there to kill us. Too bad they're all dead now. The other half of our team, our command structure, was based at Incirlik. Not anymore, though. You see, the director of the CIA showed up, hit them with some bogus charge, and took them away."

"Why would he do that?" Laura asked.

Cara nodded. "I like your wife, Brooks. She's like me. She wants to know the fucking truth."

"I had nothing to do with it."

"You were complicit."

He went silent once more.

Brick said to Laura, "You see, Mrs. Brooks, a while back, we got on the wrong side of a bunch of assholes known as the Cabal. We kind of upset their plans, and this is their way of stopping us from interfering. You know that the President was killed?"

Laura nodded.

"That was them."

"That was all planned by the chairman of—"

Brick shook his head. "No. That was their means of getting him out of the way."

"I don't believe it."

"Tell her, Colonel," Cara ordered.

He said nothing.

Cara leveled her M17 at his forehead. "Tell her."

"They'll kill her," he pleaded.

Cara shifted her aim to Laura. "I'll fucking kill her if you don't."

"All right. All right. Don't shoot."

"Talk, you son of a bitch."

"Brewer just showed up. He told me what he wanted to do and that I was to give him all the help he needed, or—"

"Or what?"

"Or they were going to kill Laura."

"So you folded like a shit poker hand," Cara growled.

"You don't understand. These people…they're everywhere. There's no hiding from them."

"You fucking asshole," Laura shouted.

"I did it to keep you safe."

"Screw you."

"You can fight about it later," Cara told them. "I want to know where they were taken."

"To some prison in Ankara. All except one who got away. Their computer guy."

"Don't worry about him." Cara looked at Brick. "Time to go."

The sound of a vehicle pulling up outside reached their ears. "Kill the light," Brick said as he hurried to the living room window and looked out.

Cara found the switch and killed the light. "What is it?"

"Two men getting out of an SUV."

"Are you expecting anyone?" Cara asked Laura Brooks.

"No."

"Looks like you've both become liabilities," Cara said. "Kill the rest of the lights and go to the bathroom."

"Give me a gun," Brooks said. "I can help."

"I'm not risking the chance that you turn on us and we get backshot. Get in the bathroom. Brick, unlock the door. We'll let them come to us."

Brooks and Laura did as instructed, the woman bearing up remarkably well, considering what she had just been told. Brick went to the front door and unlatched the lock, then fell in beside Cara, who was crouched behind the sofa, prepared and waiting for the latest arrivals.

They were good. The intruders moved like ninjas, entering the house silently. It wasn't until they were in the living room that Cara heard them. Even then, it wasn't much—just the faint whisper of fabric brushing against itself.

Cara tapped Brick on the shoulder and they rose simultaneously, weapons trained forward. The two intruders were framed against the backdrop of the large living room window, the soft moonlight filtering through silhouetting them perfectly.

Their M17s opened fire together, continuing their deafening noise until both targets were down. Cara and Brick stepped out from behind the sofa and checked the two intruders. Brick moved across the room and flicked on a lamp to give greater visibility, now able to make out the shooters clearly. Cara checked them for distinguishing marks. Both had tattoos of skulls on their forearms. She looked at Brick. "You see anything like this before?"

Brick nodded. "Hunter Killers."

"What?"

"They were a band of elite soldiers utilized by the CIA a few years back. They did a lot of wet work. Recruited from all branches of the Special Forces."

"Can we come out now?" Laura asked.

Cara nodded. "I suggest you both go back to the base and stay there. I also suggest, ma'am, that you stay far away from this asshole if you want to keep living."

"Don't worry about that."

Cara and Brick had started toward the door when Laura called after them. "Good luck, Marine."

Cara stopped and looked back. Laura smiled. "Takes one to know one."

"You too, ma'am."

Ankara, Turkey

The house looked like it had been transplanted from the US, reminiscent of a California Craftsman, just like any you might find in suburban America. Two floors, shiplap exterior, large windows, gabled roof, and a large porch. It was hidden behind a set of massive wooden double gates and had a well-maintained garden. The lights were on inside, as well as a couple of exterior ones. There were security cameras on the front gates, and it didn't take Swift long to hook into the ones that were spread around the grounds.

"Whoever set up this system needs poking in the eyes with a sharp stick," the computer tech growled. "It's a total shit show."

"Can you shut it down?" Kane asked.

"I can go one better than that. I'll put it on a loop, and whoever is watching it won't have any idea."

"Do it."

Kane, Knocker, and Axe had changed into their combat gear and were ready to insert. Slick would monitor everything from his position and warn them if they needed to get out fast. Once they had secured the house, they would call him in so he could look through their database.

Kane said, "Once we're secure, I need you to see if you can find anything regarding the team. We will be busy questioning our friend. Also, there is one other thing I want you to do."

"What's that?"

Kane told him. "I can do that."

"Good man."

A minute later, the security feed was done. "All yours, Reaper."

"See you on the other side, Slick."

They exited the Land Rover and made their way to the infiltration point they had decided upon earlier. Climbing over the fence, they dropped silently into the yard.

"You don't suppose these tossers have motion sensors, do you?" Knocker asked as though it was an afterthought.

"If there were, Slick would have told us," Kane replied.

"Perhaps we should send Axe ahead, just in case."

"Perhaps you're very funny, Limey."

"Just remember, we disarm, not kill," Kane reminded them.

"If they shoot at us, Reaper, I'm fucking shooting back," Axe growled, patting his SAW.

"Move out."

Axe led them through the shadows toward the house. They approached from the back and waited near a stone-built wall at the rear of the pool. "Slick, you copy?"

"Copy, Reaper."

"How are we looking?"

"I've got two in the living room, one in the kitchen, one in a bedroom, and one in what seems to be a basement."

"Can you see our guy anywhere?"

"He could be the one in the basement. There's no camera down there."

"Let me know if it changes."

"Roger that."

"Knocker, you're up."

The SAS man said nothing, just climbed over the rock wall and moved stealthily toward the rear of the house. He skirted the pool, his boots soundless on the sandstone paving surrounding it. After ascending the three steps from the pool area, he hurried toward the rear door.

Keeping low, Knocker tried the handle and found it unlocked. He whispered into his comms, "Talk to me, Slick."

"Hold, Reaper Three. The tango in the kitchen is facing your way."

The SAS man took in deep breaths and waited. After what seemed like an interminably long minute, Swift said, "He's sitting at the table, facing away from you."

Knocker released his 416 and passed it to Axe, then removed his M17 from the holster and eased the door open, praying that it wouldn't squeak and give his presence away.

When the opening was wide enough, he slipped through and crept toward the seated man.

Behind him, Kane filled the void, ready in case something happened. When Knocker was close enough, he clamped a hand over the man's mouth and pressed the gun against the nape of his neck. "Make a sound, mate, and I'll make sure it's your sodding last."

Behind Knocker, Kane and Axe entered. Kane took out a cable tie and bound the CIA officer's hands, then spoke to him in a barely audible voice. "We're not here for you, nor will we hurt you if you do the right thing. Nod if you understand."

The man nodded once.

"Good. Now you're going to stand up and walk ahead of us into the living room. Are the men in the room armed?"

Another nod.

"Let's go."

Kane escorted him into the living room, where the two CIA officers were taken completely by surprise at their appearance. Kane held a finger to his lips, the universal sign to stay quiet. Then he said, "Just relax and take out your weapons."

One of the men opened his mouth to speak, but Knocker stepped in and placed his M17 against the side of his head. "You heard the man."

They were relieved of their weapons and secured with cable-ties. Axe stayed with them while Kane and the Brit went for the next man. "Slick, I could use your guidance here," Kane said into his comms.

"Walk along the hallway to the second door on your left."

"Can you see him?"

"No."

"Shit, then how do you know he's there?"

"I saw him go in."

"Damn it, Slick—"

"Trust me, Reaper, he's in there."

As the words left Swift's mouth, the CIA officer burst from the room, gun in hand. Kane had no option but to shoot, which he did.

Buckling with a bullet in his leg, the man cried out and grabbed the wounded appendage. Kane hurried forward, swiftly kicking the dropped handgun out of the man's reach. "Damn it!"

Knocker moved past him with his M17 raised,

ready for the last CIA man, the one they were after, to appear.

He didn't let them down, appearing from farther along the hallway and snapping off a shot in Knocker's direction.

"Knocker, don't kill him," Kane shouted.

Cool under fire, Knocker took deliberate aim, even though it was against all his training, and shot at the man's lower torso. The wound might eventually kill him, but it wouldn't be quick.

The SAS man took deliberate strides to the fallen man and picked up the handgun, then rolled him over onto his back. "You won't die just yet, chum, and before you do, we want to know a few things."

"Fuck you," the man growled between breaths.

"Not nice. Didn't your dear old mother tell you to play nice with others?"

Kane said, "Who told you to blow up the car and make it look like a drone attack?"

The man spat at him. "You're all fucking dead."

Reaper frowned.

"I-I know who you are. John "Reaper" Kane."

Kane walked out to the living room where Axe had the others. "Who's in charge of this station?"

"I am," said a dark-haired man in his early forties.

"Who are you?"

"Roberts."

"Come with me."

"Who are you?"

"Just get up and come with me."

Roberts followed Kane past the first wounded CIA officer to the second. "Is this man on station normally, or is he new?"

Roberts said nothing.

"Come on, Roberts, this is important. He set off a car bomb and made it look like a damned UAV strike."

Roberts' eyes flared. His gaze snapped to Kane and asked, "Can you prove it?"

"Damned right, I can."

"Who are you?"

"The name is John Kane."

Recognition crept into the chief of station's eyes. "You're them. The ones being blamed for the whole fiasco here in Ankara."

"Listen, I'd love to give you the whole rundown, but right now, my sights are set on finding out who ordered the bombing. Slick, get in here."

"Roger, on my way."

"You're responsible," Roberts stated.

"No," Kane said with a shake of his head.

"You want me to start working on this wanker, Reaper?" Knocker asked. "He ain't got long left, but I can make it feel like forever."

Kane stared at the man, his visage revealing that he was seriously contemplating saying yes. He looked at Roberts. "We have footage of him leaving the car there the day before it exploded. We're not responsible for anything. All we did was piss off the wrong people."

"Who?"

"The Cabal. The same ones who killed Melissa Smith, your boss. The same ones who were responsible for the assassination of the President, and the same ones responsible for taking the rest of our team and giving them to the Turkish government and having them put on Death Row. You hear me?"

Roberts nodded. He was about to say something when Swift appeared. "Show him the footage," Kane ordered.

Swift showed Roberts a condensed version of what he had. Roberts looked at the dying man on the floor and snarled, "You damned fuck! What did you do, Craig?"

Craig smiled, showing blood-stained teeth. "What had to be done to get them out of the way."

Although Roberts' hands were cable-tied, he moved swiftly. Catching Kane unawares, he dragged the M17 from Kane's holster and shot the dying man in the head. "Asshole."

He calmly handed the gun back to Kane and said, "I'll help you with whatever you need."

Kane cut him loose. "I'm sorry about shooting your other man. I tried not to kill him."

Roberts nodded. "What do you want to do?"

"I was trying to find out who ordered it done, but I'm guessing it was Brewer. Did he come here?"

Roberts nodded. "Yes, and he spent a considerable amount of time talking to Craig. Then he went to Incirlik. That was when everything started. The strike, the President."

Kane nodded. "We need to get our people out of the prison they're in. Do you know where they're being held?"

Roberts shook his head. "Sorry."

"Slick, we need to buy them some time. Can you get this recording out to a news service?"

"I can try, but I'm not sure if any at home would take it."

"Leave it to me," Knocker said. "I know—"

"You know a reporter?" Axe asked.

"Rather well, Axel me old mate. The last time I saw her—"

Axe shook his head. "I don't want to know if you put your dick in her."

"Far from it, mate. She's my sister-in-law."

"You're married?" Kane blurted.

"No. I was, but now I'm divorced. Ended badly. As I was about to say, the last time I saw her, she was trying to skin me with a blade."

Axe looked at the SAS man sideways. "What for?"

"Her girlfriend was up for it, so I helped her out."

"I knew I shouldn't have asked."

"It wasn't my fault," Knocker replied with a shrug. "She found me attractive."

"Reaper, make him stop. My head hurts."

"Make the call, Knocker."

"Roger that."

Kane turned to Roberts. "Let's have a look at your man's leg."

———————

The picture came on the computer screen, and a blonde with a pretty face stared at Knocker. Her eyes widened at the sight of him, and her expression didn't bode well, so the SAS man knew he had to talk fast. "Cecily, don't cut me off, love. I need you to listen."

"Screw you, you frigging gobshite."

"It'll get you that promotion you always wanted at the BBC," he said hurriedly.

"Cutting your dick off would be a better thing to do."

"She wasn't the one for you, Cec. I did you a favor."

"Are you trying to sabotage this whole thing, Knocker?" Swift asked.

"Who's there with you, asswipe?"

Swift moved into the screen. "My name is Sam Swift, ma'am, and we really need your help. I would like to send you a video file about the drone strike in Ankara."

"Why would I watch it?" she asked.

"Because it wasn't a drone strike, you silly cow,"

Knocker said. "It was made to look like one."

"That's it, I'm gone. Screw you, Ray."

"Wait! Please wait," Swift pleaded. "Let me send it to you. Watch it, and if you think it's something, reach out to me, and I'll tell you the rest."

Cecily thought about it for a moment before saying, "Send it."

The screen went blank, and Swift turned to Knocker. "I can see why that woman dislikes you, Raymond."

"Don't you start."

"You do know if you want something from someone, you need to be nice, right?"

"That *was* nice."

A few minutes later, Cecily came back on. "All right, I'm listening."

Swift said, "The bombing in Ankara was a setup. It was a car bomb, not a drone strike. The people the Turks have in prison aren't responsible. We need to get this out there, or they'll have them executed."

"Why would they do that?"

"We pissed the wrong people off. The same ones responsible for the assassination of the President, among other things."

"Holy shite."

Knocker said, "Listen, we need you to run the footage, and that's it. Don't go digging into anything else. These tossers play for keeps, Cec. Promise me you won't."

She saw the expression on his face and knew he wasn't lying. "All right. I promise."

"Good lass."

"Ray?"

"Yes?"

Her face softened. "You be careful, OK. Just because I don't like you, it doesn't mean I want you dead."

He thought of saying something flippant but instead said, "We're good. You just watch your back. Don't stay alone."

They signed off and Knocker went in search of Kane, finding him finishing off the dressing on the wound of the CIA man he'd shot. "She's going to do it," the Brit told him.

"Good, now let's see if we can find out the location of the rest of the team before Cara and Brick get here.

CHAPTER 7

Washington, DC

Ares watched the recorded news report for the second time, then turned off the television before replacing the remote into the top drawer of the polished desk. His jaw pulsated as he ground his teeth, anger coursing through his veins. This was manageable, but it had to be gotten ahead of. The ones in prison in Turkey had to be brought home since they had links to Hank Jones. It would be easy enough to implicate them in the assassination of Carter.

There was a brief knock on the door before Paul Brewer opened it and stepped into the office, closing it behind him. Ares shot him a scathing look, and when he spoke, his voice was full of venom. "What the fuck are you going to do?"

"You mean, the BBC report?"

"Of course, I mean the damned report."

"It was released by a female reporter in the UK. She had ties to Raymond Jensen, who is part of Kane's team."

"So they found a way to fuck us over. That was careless, Paul. Why didn't someone know about the camera?"

"I have no idea."

"You're the blasted CIA. There's no excuse for you not knowing."

"We can't get everything," Brewer said abruptly.

"Watch your tone with me, Paul."

Even though the voice was low, the menacing tone was there. He nodded. "What do you want me to do about it?"

"Reach out to General Kadir. Get him to transfer the prisoners into the custody of a team you are sending to fetch them. Then release evidence that they are tied to the assassination of the President."

"You want them brought back to America and put on trial?" he asked incredulously.

"No, I want them to disappear. I do not want the plane to reach American soil, understood?"

Brewer remained silent, an uncertain expression on his face. "You want me to kill our own people?"

"Think of it as doing something for the greater good."

Brewer nodded. "I'll see to it."

"Now, what are we going to do about Mister Kane and the rest of them?"

"We could always ask Hades to send a team to Ankara. Get him to pull his weight."

"Leave me. I will see to it."

Once Brewer had vacated the office, Ares made a call.

A man with a trim goatee appeared on the display. "Ah. I was wondering when I would hear from you."

"It's time for you to go to work, Hades," Ares said. "Artemis' pitiful effort produced no results. I want you to send a team to Ankara and find Kane and his commandos."

"I will have someone on the ground in a few hours. Do you know where they are?"

"If I knew that, there would be no need for me to be making this call. They would already be frigging dead."

Hades shrugged. "No matter. Our intelligence will find them in no time."

Ares hung up. "Good fucking luck."

———————

Zulu Six, Allegheny Mountains

"Pull up, something is wrong," Hunt told Striker suddenly.

The SUV came to a halt within sight of the battered buildings of the ZULU Six camp. Hunt reached for a pair of binoculars and searched the surrounding area before he focused on the buildings.

"What is it, Bord?" Rucker asked.

"I don't know," Hunt replied. He opened the vehicle's door and slipped out of the passenger seat. "Wait here. If I don't come back, take the package and get the hell out. You too, Striker."

"Roger that."

Hunt put on his body armor and picked up the M4A1 before slipping into the trees to recon the old facility. As he circled the clearing where the structures were, he came across evidence of what had gone down: bullet casings, scars on trees, and blood trails. Then he discovered a body—one of Striker's men, the operator called Wire.

"Shit," Hunt breathed. He didn't bother to check him; he didn't need to.

Hunt moved on stealthily and soon came across Hammer. The SEAL had taken a shot in his leg and another in his head. Things weren't looking good. Lying next to an old deadfall he found Barrel, his throat cut. Whoever had hit the unused facility were top-echelon operators. It was imperative he find out what happened to the others.

Hunt broke cover and worked his way down to the building where Jones had been holed up. Finding the rear door open, he listened for several moments before moving cautiously inside.

The building was vacant, so he walked toward the open front door. It was there he found Jacks and Popeye. He looked down at his operator and sat down on the steps. "Shit, Pop, why'd you go and do that?"

He figured it had happened sometime the day before. He pressed the button on his comms and said, "Come on down, it's all clear."

When the SUV came to a stop, Hunt strode purposefully to the rear door and opened it. With a somewhat animalistic growl, he dragged Harris out of the back and dropped the mining magnate face-down in the gravel with a grunt.

Hunt turned him over with his boot, then bent down to rip the gag from the man's mouth and remove the blindfold. With the covering off, the mining magnate blinked to adjust his eyes to the light. He looked at Hunt and asked, "Where are we?"

"This is where you're going to die, asshole, unless you give me the right answers to the questions I will ask you. Do you understand me?"

"I don't know anything."

Hunt hit him hard. The mining magnate's head rocked back, and he slumped to his side.

"Bord, what's going on? Where is everyone?" Striker asked.

Hunt stared at the SEAL commander, savagery burning in his eyes. "They're dead. I found most of your men in the trees. Popeye and Jacks are behind the concrete there. The signs of a fucking firefight are everywhere."

Striker turned pale. "All of my men?"

"I don't know. I couldn't find Anvil or the general. Maybe they took them, maybe they got away."

Hunt saw that the SEAL had been affected by the loss of his friend. "Rucker?"

He looked at Hunt.

"I want you to see if you can find out where the others went—"

"We're here."

They turned as one at the sound of the voice, relieved to see Anvil and the general walking toward them, looking like they'd had a rough time. "What happened, Matt?" Striker asked.

"They came out of nowhere. They were on us before we even knew."

Anvil related what had gone down from beginning to end. Once he finished, Striker patted him on the shoulder and said, "You did good, Matt. The general was the mission, and you kept him alive."

"You know I'm here, right?" Jones growled. He pointed at Harris. "Now for this asshole."

"He might be our ticket to some answers," Hunt explained. "Let's get him inside."

Once they relocated into the cabin, Hunt shoved Harris into a chair and tied him to it. With that done, he turned to Rucker and Anvil. "You two outside and eyes open."

"Where do you want to start, Bord?" Striker asked after the others left.

"General, maybe you should go too."

"The hell you say. I'm right here all the way."

Hunt stood in front of Harris and stated, "I want names."

"What?"

"I want names. Let's start with who Ares is."

Harris shook his head. "I don't know."

Hunt took his handgun from its holster and shot him in the leg just above the kneecap. Harris howled and jerked wildly, trying to free himself from his bonds. The SEAL chief grabbed the man's hair and pulled his head up, bringing his face close to look him in his tear-filled eyes. "Listen, motherfucker, those men out there were ours, and I'm done pissing about. Start talking, or I'm just going to fill you with so many holes you'll bleed to death real slow."

Harris dejectedly stared at him in pain-filled silence.

"Right, let's start with Ares again. Who?"

"I don't know," the mining magnate pleaded.

BLAM!

This time it was the other leg, and Harris' screech was so high-pitched it sounded like a monkey in the jungle.

"Who is Ares?" Hunt shouted.

"All right! All right! Don't shoot me again."

"Talk."

"I don't know who Ares is. I only know the lieutenants."

"Who?"

"Me, Paul Brewer, Leyland Meyers, and Thomas Winkler."

Hunt snapped a glance at Hank Jones. The general stepped forward. "Is that it?"

"Yes."

"I thought Ares was Carter?"

"He was until they retired him. Attracted too much attention."

Jones nodded. "Who knows who Ares is now?"

"Paul Brewer."

"Can you get in touch with him?"

"Y-yes."

"Chief, Striker, a minute," Jones said.

They followed the general outside and Jones turned to look at them, his face grim. "What are your plans once we get what we need from that ass?"

Hunt shrugged. "I don't know. Never thought that far ahead."

"We can't leave him alive," Jones said.

"You want us to kill him?"

Jones shook his head. "No, Chief, I'll do it. I want to send those bastards a message."

Hunt looked at Striker, and the SEAL commander nodded. Hunt took out his weapon and gave it to Jones. "There's one in the pipe."

The three returned to the interior of the cabin and walked over to Harris. Blood had formed a pool under the chair where he sat. Hunt took out the cell they'd taken from Harris when they'd kidnapped him, turned it on, and gave it to the mining magnate. "Call Brewer."

With bloody, trembling hands, Harris pressed the series of buttons. Hunt said, "Put it on video call."

Jones moved to stand behind Harris. "Hold it so he can see both of us."

A picture of Brewer appeared. "What do you want...okay. Look who we have here. To what do I owe the pleasure, General?"

"Just wanted to let you know I'm still around, and for you to tell Ares this isn't over. I'm coming for you, asshole, and hell will be coming with me."

"Brave talk for an old man," Brewer tormented.

"Not too old to frag your ass. Our friend here gave us the names of the lieutenants. We know who you are. So—get this—every one of you has a target painted on your back. Big ones."

"You scare me, old man."

"You *should* be scared, Brewer."

Jones raised the weapon in his hand so the CIA director could see it. Then he shot Harris in the back of the head, the phone falling from limp hands and clattering to the boards at his feet.

Hunt reached down and retrieved the cell from on the floor. He turned it over and looked at Brewer, who was still glaring at the screen on his end. The SEAL chief said, "See you in hell, motherfucker."

Then he hung up.

"We need somewhere to lay up," Jones said.

Striker frowned. "I thought we were going after—"

"No, we need to find somewhere to hide for a while until the heat is off us. Somewhere we can regroup, and I can reach out to Alex Joseph."

Striker nodded. "I know a place."

Washington, DC

There was venom in Ares' voice when he was informed of the assassination of Solomon Harris. The whole plan was meant to be simple: gather up everyone and kill them, no survivors. These people were proving more resourceful than expected, and it was pissing Ares off no end.

"The call originated from the place called Zulu Six. I had White double back to it, and they found Harris still tied to the chair. Jones and those with him were gone."

"This was meant as a warning for me?" Ares hissed.

Brewer nodded.

"How hard can it be to find these people?"

"They're good at what they do. Well-trained, well-equipped."

"I don't care what they are. You tell your Mister White to find Jones and the others, or I'll have his goddamned head."

Brewer nodded. "What about the team you sent to Turkey?"

"They'll land in a few hours. It'll be early hours of the morning and easier to get them out under cover of darkness. I reached out to my head of station and told him the team was inbound."

"Will he be a problem?"

"No. He's a sheep. He'll do whatever I say."

"Good."

CHAPTER 8

Ankara, Turkey

Kane stood staring at Roberts, who had just related the content of the call from Brewer. He considered what it meant for Bravo team for a moment. "The news story must have worked. Now they can't afford for them to be executed, so they're taking them home."

"Don't be so sure. The story he gave me was that they're linked to the assassination of the President," Roberts explained. "If you ask me, they're not going to see the shores of the US."

"You think they'll kill them?" Cara asked.

"They can't afford for them to speak to anyone," Roberts replied.

Kane agreed. "We can use this to our advantage. We will hit the convoy while it's on the move."

"Why not do it at the airfield?" Knocker asked.

"It's out in the open that way while they're being transferred to the plane from the transport."

Kane looked at Roberts. "What is the airfield like?"

"Small, private, just like the CIA uses."

"Do you have any night vision capability?"

"A little."

"Cara, take a look. If it's good, we'll do it at the airfield."

"Roger that."

"Slick, find out what you can about the airfield."

"On it, Reaper."

Kane looked at Knocker. "I don't suppose you have a friend who can help get us out of the country?"

"As a matter of fact, I do."

"It'll need to be straight after we extract the team."

"Now you're stretching the friendship. Leave it with me."

"I'm relying on you, Knocker."

"I'm that type of guy."

"Shit, get out of here."

———

"The night vision gear is all good, Reaper," Cara said. "I've been thinking, and I'd say that there'll be some kind of lighting on the tarmac that will help those with."

"OK. Let's look at this place," he said, pointing at a satellite picture on a screen. "We've got buildings here, here, and here." He indicated the second one. "If you set up here, it'll give you a full field of fire."

"Looks good to me."

"The rest of us will come at them from behind this building here." Kane stabbed a finger at the picture.

"They will more than likely have guards out," Roberts suggested.

"We'll deal with them."

"Try not to kill them, Kane. They're not all like Craig was."

"We'll do our best," Kane allowed. "Speaking of Craig, did Brewer ask about him?"

"Yes. I said he was out."

"And he bought that?"

"Yes. He told me to tell him to be on the plane."

"I guess he was a loose end too."

"Looks that way."

Kane said, "We've got just over an hour until they touch down. Time to get ready."

———————

Ferrero climbed to his feet, stretching as best he could to work the kink out of his back. He was sick and tired of waiting and just wished they would start the farce of a trial so they could have their chance at escape. He, Arenas, and Teller had discussed many options over the past days, none of which seemed feasible. That left the trial.

"You OK, Luis?" Teller asked.

"Yes, just can't sleep."

"You're not the only one. I don't think I've had a decent night's sleep since we've been here. I blame the room service."

They all chuckled. "Yeah, it's pretty shit."

"What do you suppose they did with the general?" Arenas asked.

"I don't know," Ferrero replied. Actually, he'd stopped thinking about it because he was continuously coming back with the same answer: she was more than likely dead.

Noise from outside the cells in the hallway drew their attention. Lights came on, and then they heard the rattle of keys in the lock. The door swung open, and a guard entered. "You are leaving."

"What? Where are we going?" Ferrero asked.

"You're going home to be put on trial," a man in a suit said as he entered the cell. "All of you."

"Who are you?"

"Wells. FBI."

"What are we being tried for?" Ferrero asked.

"Conspiracy to assassinate the President for a start. Depending on what we find out, possibly more."

"You're shitting me!" Ferrero exclaimed in disbelief.

"I bet you wish I were. Turn around and face the wall."

"Screw you."

"Your alternative is to stay here if you want."

Grudgingly, the three turned. They were all handcuffed and escorted into the hall where the others, General Kadir, and four more FBI agents waited. Ferrero turned to Wells. "What about General Thurston?"

"I don't have anything about a General Thurston."

"You must have; she was locked up with us. They took her away and didn't bring her back."

Wells looked at Kadir. "Thurston?"

"There was no one else."

Ferrero lunged at him. "You lying son of a bitch. She was here. What did you do to her?"

Wells and another agent grabbed him by the arms, dragging him back. "Settle down, this doesn't help."

"Screw you. She was here, and now we're just going to leave?"

"Get moving, Ferrero, or I'll put your sorry ass back in that cell you smell so much like."

Ferrero stopped and reined in his temper. He pushed his anger to the back of his mind but vowed that it wasn't over. Not by a long shot.

When he drew level with Reynolds and Morales, he asked them how they were holding up.

"I'm fine," Reynolds replied.

"Me too," said Morales. "Being cooped up like that gave us a lot of girl time to catch up."

Ferrero nodded.

"We're not leaving without Mary, are we?" the doctor asked.

"It looks that way, but we'll be back. Don't worry, we'll find her."

They were herded outside and put into a waiting truck, with an additional six of Kadir's guards riding escort in another vehicle. They were there to deliver them to the airfield and wait until they departed.

Once aboard, the trucks fired up with loud roars, blowing clouds of black diesel fumes behind them. Both lurched forward as they commenced the journey along a rough street filled with holes toward their destination. The drive would take them twenty minutes. From there, they would be loaded onto the plane for their doomed voyage home.

———————

"Reaper, I have two trucks inbound, over."

"Copy, Reaper Two. Stand by."

The team was in place before the plane landed and its occupants disembarked. The Bombardier Global 6000 sat quietly on the tarmac, with two guards at the steps and the pilots sitting in the cockpit, waiting for their return flight. The night air was cold and clear, the moon overhead lighting the landscape adequately.

Kane said into his comms. "Reaper Three and Five, stand by."

One of the guards at the steps moved slightly.

"Reaper Three and Five, copy." They had waited while the plane was being refueled before they had taken it.

"Cara, ETA?"

"Two mikes, Reaper."

It was the longest two minutes of Kane's life. It passed slower than molasses being tipped from a tin on a cold day. Then, as though someone had taken the video player off slow motion, the trucks roared into view, their lights blazing.

They pulled up a short distance from the plane on the tarmac, placing themselves between Brick and Knocker and the rest of the team. "Cara, do you have visual?"

"Roger."

"OK, let's move. The soldiers first. Execute."

Kane and Axe hurried toward the trucks with their suppressed weapons up to their shoulders. At the rear of the second truck, the six Turkish soldiers were jumping down. One saw Kane and Axe on approach, and he let out a yelp of alarm and fought to bring his weapon up. Kane swiftly brought him to his knees with two 5.56 rounds to his chest. Beside him, Axe shot a second soldier with his SAW.

"Knocker, Brick, now," Kane snapped into his

comms.

On the opposite side of the trucks at the steps of the plane, Reapers Three and Five moved with practiced precision. Their M17s came up and they picked their targets. Four shots and two of the remaining guards fell to the tarmac.

On the hangar roof, Cara squeezed the trigger on the CSASS and felt its comforting recoil. One of the final two soldiers fell like a marionette with its strings cut.

Stunned by the brutal swiftness of what had just happened to his comrades, the soldier dropped his weapon and threw his arms up. *"Ateş etmeyin! Ateş etmeyin!"*

"Move on the first truck," Kane ordered.

The FBI men had no idea what was happening. Two were out of the first truck, and they were taken by surprise. By the time they drew their weapons, they were staring down the cavernous barrels of Knocker's and Brick's handguns. "Oh, bollocks," the SAS man said to the gaping FBI men. "I bet you feel like right plonkers about now, huh, Guv?"

Brick shrugged. "I don't know what he just said, but I bet you are."

Kane and Axe appeared behind them. "The rest of you in the truck, get out."

The first person to appear was Wells, who climbed from the cab along with the driver. They walked to the rear of the truck. He looked at Kane and said, "I hope you know who you're fucking with?" he said angrily. "We're the FBI."

The flat slap of a suppressed weapon sounded, and an armed Turk with a weapon fell near the second truck. "I think you missed the driver, Reaper," Cara remarked.

Knocker said, "Looks like the CIA didn't want to off their own guys."

"What are you talking about?"

"Reaper, is that you?" Ferrero called from the rear of the truck.

"It's me, Luis. Come on out."

Before long, all of Bravo, minus Thurston, were greeting their friends. The FBI agents were stood to one side. "It is good to see you, *amigo*," Arenas said to Brick. "I was thinking you maybe forget about us."

"Not by a long shot, Carlos."

Kane stared at Wells. "We're taking our friends, but I'll give you some advice for free. Don't fly that plane home. You won't make it."

"What do you mean?" Wells snapped. "Where are my men?"

"Everyone is in the cabin, and what I mean is that this plane was never meant to make it back to the States. These people, our friends, are marked for death. You lot are also expendable."

"How do you know this?"

"You ever heard of the Cabal, Wells?" Ferrero asked. "We have. We kind of pissed them off.

That's how we ended up on a bogus charge in a Turkish prison."

"That's why you're being transported back to the States. For conspiracy to assassinate the President."

"That was the Cabal," Kane told him. "Brick, check the plane. Knocker, help him."

Kane continued, "We were the ones who released the video footage of the car bomb to the BBC."

Wells raised his eyebrows. "You?"

"Yeah. Who told you to come here? To make the pickup?"

"We got a call from Paul Brewer at the CIA."

"Do you ever get orders from the CIA?"

Wells frowned. "Not as such. Usually, it is from our own boss or Justice."

"Brewer's part of it," Ferrero told him.

Wells shook his head. "This is the biggest shit sandwich anyone has ever tried to feed me."

"I don't care if you believe us," Kane growled. "But hear this: the only reason you and your people are still alive is that we figure that you have no idea what's going on."

Knocker appeared in the doorway of the plane. "Found it, Reaper."

"Go and have a look," Kane told Wells. "Or one of your men. We've got a little time."

Wells nodded at one of his agents. The man hesitated until Kane said, "It's OK. Go."

The man hurried to the plane steps and followed

Knocker. Brick emerged and walked over to where they all stood. "It's set to go off about the time they're halfway over the Atlantic."

"You mean, there's a bomb on the plane?" Wells asked.

The bearded ex-SEAL stared at him. "Bet your ass there is."

Knocker and the other FBI agent emerged from the plane. They rejoined the group, and the agent nodded at his boss. "They were telling the truth, sir. This is all fucked up. They saved our lives."

"Reaper, we've got movement. You need to get out of there. Now."

"Roger."

Kane looked at his people. "Gear up, we've got company."

"What's going on?" Wells asked.

"Our overwatch picked up movement. If I were you, I'd come with us. I have a feeling those guys are hostiles."

Knocker and Brick grabbed their primary weapons and discarded the FBI coats. "Get into the trucks. Cara, we'll pick you up on the way out." Kane ordered. "Are you coming, Wells?"

The FBI SAC nodded. "We're right behind you."

"Too late, Reaper," Cara's voice was loud in his ear. The smack of the suppressed CSASS came out of the darkness.

The night came alive with automatic gunfire and

muzzle flashes winking in the darkness.

"The hangar," Kane shouted. "Get to the hangar."

They started running across the tarmac toward the large metal building, the FBI men bringing up the rear. Bullet strikes chased them across the open ground until they caught up with the trailing FBI agent.

5.56 rounds from German Heckler and Koch G36Ks hammered into the tail-end man, knocking him off his feet. He cried out as he cartwheeled over the rough tarmac, sliding to a halt in an untidy heap.

"Put some fire on those assholes," Kane shouted as he brought up his 416.

Ahead of him, Axe, Knocker, and Brick followed suit, while Bravo and the rest of the FBI agents kept running.

"Cara, how many do you see?" Kane asked, firing at the winking muzzle flashes.

"There's a company at least, Reaper," she said desperately. "Get out of there."

A shout brought his head around. A second FBI agent was down. Crouched over him was Morales as she tried to help. Another agent stopped to give her a hand and slumped beside her when a bullet punched into his head.

"Shit," Kane swore. "Brick, get Morales out of there."

"Roger that." The big SEAL ran across the tarmac toward the doctor.

Kane changed out a magazine. Beside him, a loud grunt drew his attention, and he saw Axe collapse to his knees. "Axe."

Kane knelt, knowing the whole show was turning to shit. "Axe, where are you hit?"

"Son of a bitch got me in the fucking armor. I'll be fine. Just give me a moment."

"We don't have a moment."

At that point, Knocker was the only one, apart from Cara, keeping them covered. Kane knew it was only a matter of time before one of his team went down for good, especially with the SAW out of action.

"Let me help you, *amigo*," Arenas said, relieving Axe of his primary weapon. Soon he had the light machine gun operating again and was laying down good fire.

Kane helped Axe to his feet, and they began moving toward the hangar. They passed the two fallen FBI agents and kept on. Behind them, Knocker and Arenas continued their rate of fire until they all made it to cover.

Kane said into his comms, "Slick, you there, buddy?"

"What's going on?"

"You need to find us a way out of here. We're taking fire from a company-sized force."

The attackers started to close on the hangar. From above them, Cara tried to pick off as many as she could. Arenas kept firing Axe's SAW, which was doing the trick, but for how long?

"Axe, are you OK?" Kane shouted.

"I'm fine." He came to his feet from where he was resting and took out his M17 to join the fight.

"Reaper One, Bravo Four, over."

"Copy, Bravo Four."

"You need to hear this."

"Send it."

"Team eins, nach rechts. Team zwei, links. Team drei, Das Feuer abdeckt—"

"They're German," Kane said. "What the fuck are German troops doing here?"

"Give you one guess."

"Damn it, find us a way out."

"Fall back to the rear, Reaper until you reach the road. You need to go now before they encircle you."

"Copy that," Kane called. "We're falling back. Brick, on point. Take Carlos with you."

"Roger."

Arenas hurried over to Axe and offered him the SAW. "Here, *amigo*."

Axe took the weapon and handed him his M17 and two spare magazines. "Keep your head down, Carlos."

Brick and Carlos led them all out the back of the hangar. Kane and Knocker remained behind to provide cover. "Cara, go with the rest."

"Moving."

Bullets pounded the sheet metal walls of the hangar with an irregular staccato rhythm. Knocker looked at Kane and grinned. "This is fun."

Bullets cut through the opening close to both of them.

The SAS man fired through the open door and saw an attacker fall. "You think we should go, Colonel?"

"Yes," shouted Kane. "Follow me."

They ran across the large expanse of concrete floor and out the rear of the hangar, following the others.

CHAPTER 9

Ankara, Turkey

Hauptmann Bruno Wagner barked orders into his comms and watched his men of the *Kommando Spezialkräfte* execute them with trained precision. His problem appeared to be that the force they were facing were just as well trained as his men.

"*Leutnant* Berger, do you read me, over?"

"Yes, sir," Berger replied.

"Push your men farther around to the right. Try and get behind them to cut off any escape."

"Yes, sir."

Why the blue-eyed, blond-haired Wagner and his commandos were in Turkey, he didn't know. They'd never done anything like this before—a covert insertion in a country that was a NATO ally, to remain covert and then get out as quickly as possible. *What* they were doing Wagner had no questions about.

They were to find a team of mercenaries that posed a threat to European stability, had killed a French team of "soldiers," and terminate them with extreme prejudice. In other words, no loose ends.

Not a simple operation as had been thought, for now he had battle casualties, both killed and wounded.

Suddenly the firing from the hangar stopped. Wagner frowned then realized what was happening. "No, no, no. *Scheiße!* All teams close in on the hangar. Move, move."

With his G36K up to his shoulder, Wagner rushed forward, ready to fire if he needed to. The German commandos converged on the hangar and found it empty. The captain swore when he saw this and turned his hot gaze on the man nearest to him. "*Feldwebel* Ludwig, take your team and find them. We'll be close behind."

"Yes, sir," the sergeant snapped. He barked orders, and five men fell in behind him.

Wagner turned to Berger. "You and your men gather our wounded and dead. No one gets left behind. We were never here."

"Yes, sir."

"The rest of you follow me."

———

"Reaper, I found a way for you to extract," Swift said.

"Don't keep me hanging, Bravo Four," Kane

growled.

"Approximately five hundred meters ahead of you, you'll find a bus depot. It's the best I can do. From there, you're on your own. I need to get to the RV, or when you all haul ass out of this country, I'll be left behind."

"Roger that. Good luck."

"I have a feeling you'll need it more than me, Reaper. Bravo Four out."

"Reaper Five, copy?"

"Read you Lima Charlie, Reaper."

"There's a bus depot ahead. We're stopping there."

"Does that mean what I think it does?" Brick asked.

"Roger."

"Shit. Copy, we'll stop there."

"What's going on, Reaper?" Ferrero asked Kane.

"We're going to catch a bus."

———————

About seven minutes later, the group reached the bus depot, and Kane ordered them to set up a small perimeter while Knocker worked on getting a bus started. Cara turned to Brick and said, "Time to use your muscles, Big Boy. Help me up onto one of the buses."

The roof of the bus afforded her a clear view in the direction they'd just come from. Her scope swept left and right, trying to pick up any indication they were being followed. It wasn't long before she spotted movement.

"Reaper, we've got visitors," Cara said calmly into her comms.

"How many, Reaper Two?"

"There's six of them coming along the street we came in on."

"OK, Slow them down. Brick, Axe, incoming from the west."

On top of the bus, Cara let out a slow, steady breath and squeezed the trigger on the CSASS. The flat slap of the weapon was audible from above. The single shot brought forth a stream of gunfire from the remaining shooters.

From beside the bus, Axe opened up with the SAW and sprayed the advancing team of Germans with deadly fire. It drove them to cover, where they tried to suppress the incoming fire with heavy return fire of their own.

Meanwhile, Knocker was under the hood, trying to start the bus they were to leave in. "How much longer, Knocker?" Kane asked.

"I'm not part of Louis Hamilton's pit crew, you know. It'll go when it goes."

"Who?" Kane asked, regretting his question before it left his lips.

"Louis Hamilton. Formula One racing car driver?"

"Just get the bus going, Knocker."

"You mean, you've never heard of him?"

"Knocker, the bus."

Knocker shook his head and mumbled to himself, "Bloody heathens, the lot of you. I suppose you've never heard of football either."

"LA Galaxy," Reynolds said, "Now move the fuck over."

Reynolds squeezed in beside him and went to work. A couple of minutes later, she looked at him and said, "Get in, and I'll try it."

Knocker ran around and jumped in the driver's seat. "OK."

"Pump the gas."

Knocker did as he was told, and Reynolds tinkered with something quickly which turned the motor over. The bus roared to life, and Reynolds slammed the hood shut. Ferrero shouted, "Everyone on board."

Kane ordered the others to fall back, and as they did, the rest of the German commandos came out of the darkness, firing.

The last person aboard was Cara, who rushed for the rear seat with her weapon. As she arrived at the back of the bus, the whole rear window blew out. She lunged forward, hitting the padded seat with a grunt, and shouted, "Get down! Axe, get your ass back here."

"She's bossy, isn't she," Brick said to him.

"It's an officer thing."

"Now, Marine."

Axe hefted his SAW and worked his way to the back of the bus. The vehicle lurched forward before he was ready, making him lunge to get his balance, almost sending him out the rear window opening. Cara grabbed his belt and hauled him back to safety.

"Where the hell do you think you're going?"

"Thought I might stay behind, ma'am, and join those boys for Oktoberfest."

"I'll buy you a beer when we get back home," Cara promised as more rounds hammered into the back of the bus. "In the meantime, get that frigging SAW working."

A few moments later, the suppressed SAW rattled to life and sprayed their attackers with deadly fire. The bus roared as Knocker changed gears, giving it gas in great bursts. A cloud of diesel smoke blew out of the exhaust as it gathered speed, the smokescreen obscuring their view from the back of the bus. The lumbering behemoth blew through a fence and out of the depot, turned left, and disappeared into the darkness.

Behind them, Wagner came to a stop, and his men ceased fire. A bitter curse escaped his lips, and he turned to his sergeant. "Get the men together. This isn't finished."

"Are you sure you don't want to come with us?" Kane asked Wells over the roar of the Airbus A400M Atlas. "It'll probably be safer than heading back to the States at the moment."

Wells shook his head. "We'll hang out with the CIA boys for a while so I can reach out to our director."

"Just be careful who you trust."

The FBI agent in charge nodded. "I'm beholden to you for what you've done for us."

"Before we go," Ferrero said. "Are you sure there were no orders about the general?"

"She wasn't even on the list."

Ferrero's face was grim as he looked at Kane. "We need to find her, Reaper."

"We will. You can count on it."

They said their goodbyes and were about to get on the plane when Roberts appeared. "I just got a report of flash traffic coming through about you guys. It seems Interpol wants you now. You've been put on the terrorist watch list by your country."

"Those guys don't believe in half measures," Kane said with a smile. "Well, once we get our commanding officer back, those assholes are in for a rude shock. See you stateside for a beer when this is all done, Roberts. Thanks for your help."

"Call on us any time you need help, Kane."

Kane and Ferrero walked toward the Atlas. As they climbed the rear loading ramp, they were met by a man in a suit. "Welcome aboard. Are you the last?"

Kane nodded.

"Great. The name is Covington."

"Thanks for your help," Ferrero said to the man, who had a British accent.

"No worries, old chap. Had I not assisted, Jensen would probably have paid me a visit on some dark lonely night. Anyway, have a seat, and we'll get you to Austria."

Kane glanced at Ferrero. "I'll say this about Knocker; he sure knows a lot of people."

Five minutes later, the Royal Air Force Atlas was lifting into the sky, on its way to Austria, where the team could regroup and reassess. Then their mission was to find Thurston, wherever she was.

———————

Washington, DC

It was late in the evening when word came through to Ares, who was still working. The Cabal commander looked down at the vibrating phone on the desk, picked it up, and said, "Mister Brewer, I assume you have something to report?"

The ensuing silence signified that there was no easy way of saying it. Best to rip the Band-aid off and deal with the fallout afterward. "Everything went to shit in Turkey."

Ares placed the pen on the sheet of paper and sighed heavily into the encrypted cell phone. There was a period of drawn-out silence with eyes closed as Ares digested the news, tapping the desk with nervous energy. Then, "Tell me what happened."

"Reaper Team was waiting at the plane for the transfer of the prisoners. They killed the Turkish guards."

"What about the FBI team you dispatched?"

"That's where things get crazy. The Germans showed up, and a firefight ensued. Three of the FBI people were killed, along with some of the Commandos. Kane and all the others got away to a bus depot and stole a bus. The FBI people were with them."

"What do you mean, 'with them?'"

"The German troop commander said they all seemed to be working together."

"Does this get any fucking better?" Ares asked bitterly.

"They've disappeared. We have no idea where they are."

"Then, Paul, you'd better find them."

"We're working on it."

Ares looked at the clock on the wall, which told him it was a little after nine. "Get over here now. Bring that folder you've been keeping set aside for a rainy day."

"We're doing it now?" Brewer asked.

"Yes, we are. Before this all gets out of hand. Once it's in motion, it'll be harder to stop. I'll reach out to Winkler."

"All right, I'll see you soon."

The White House, Washington, DC

President Richard Nelson stared at the three people seated in front of him: CIA Director Paul Brewer, Chairman of the Joint Chiefs General Thomas Winkler, and Speaker of the House Clarissa Rhodes. He looked at his watch for the third time in a minute, and the result was still the same: ten-thirty. He shifted his gaze back to them and asked, "Is someone going to tell me what this is about?"

"Sir," Clarissa said, "Paul has more disturbing intelligence about Russian interference in Ukraine."

"Miss Rhodes, I already have a proposal on my desk about Ukraine. I'm not finished looking it over yet."

"I appreciate that, sir, but if you would just have a look."

Nelson sighed.

"We wouldn't disturb you if it wasn't important."

"Where is Harvey?"

"We were unable to reach the SECDEF, sir," Clarissa lied.

"All right," Nelson said grudgingly. "Give me a look at it."

Brewer passed the folder over, and Nelson opened it and started flicking through the contents. Clarissa said, "As you can see, sir, the Russians have moved in anti-air missiles, tanks, and Sukhoi Su-35s, and there are reports of at least three divisions moving closer to the border, with an additional five on high alert."

Nelson snapped his gaze up to stare at Winkler. "Is this true?"

"It's what intelligence is telling us, sir," the general replied.

"How long has this been happening?"

"It's been happening ever since the…since President Carter was assassinated," Brewer told him.

Nelson's jaw dropped. "Why am I just hearing about this now? I've heard not a word at morning intelligence meetings."

"We thought they were just posturing, sir. Maybe seeing how you would react. They usually do something like this after a new President comes into office," Winkler explained.

"What is different this time, General?" Nelson snapped.

"We believe the Russians have moved another mechanized division into the forest in Eastern Ukraine."

"You have to be kidding me!" Nelson exclaimed, stunned. "Why would they do that?"

"It all points to them taking over the rest of Ukraine, sir," Winkler said. "If we move now and move decisively, we might be able to deter them."

"By move decisively, I assume you mean American forces?"

Winkler nodded. "I expect that if we act, the Germans, French, and British will come with us."

"You expect? What if the Russians take no notice of *our* posturing, General? What then?"

Winkler glanced at Clarissa, who gave him an almost imperceptible nod. He looked earnest. "Then we have to stop them, sir, and drive them back from the frontier."

"You mean, start a war?"

"If that is what it takes," the general replied. "Sir, if we allow them to take Ukraine, we feel they might drive down into Romania to boost their gas and oil reserves. After that, Belarus, Lithuania, and others will follow."

Nelson raised his hands and massaged his temples. "Oh, God, what next?"

"It calls for decisive action, Mister President," Clarissa said in a quietly authoritative voice."

Nelson nodded. "Who do you suggest, General?"

"We could deploy the Second Cavalry from Germany right away, sir. The 173rd Airborne Brigade Combat Team from Italy. That would give us numbers on the ground quickly and time to deploy the First Armored Division and the First and Second Divisions, sir. Once we have air power and the main NATO countries fall in with us, we can hit the Russians hard."

"I thought this was a defensive move, General?" Nelson queried. "That it was only to deter the Russians?"

"We're almost certain they mean to invade, sir. Call it a preemptive strike."

Once more, Nelson's face was deeply etched with stress lines. "I don't know. Maybe we should try diplomatic channels first."

"They will willingly talk, sir, I can guarantee it," Winkler said. "And while they're doing that, they'll be slipping more troops into Eastern Ukraine. Sir—"

"Could you give me some time alone with the President, gentlemen?" Clarissa said.

They looked confused but nodded and rose, adjusting their suits as they exited the office, leaving Clarissa alone with Nelson. He looked at her. "What should I do, Clarissa?"

"Winkler is right, Richard," she said softly. "Should you fail to act, the Russian president will consider you weak."

"But all those men. If war breaks out—"

Clarissa came to her feet, trying to mask the disdain she felt for the man before her. She'd spent too long on this—on him—to lose it now. She walked around behind him and laid her hands on his shoulders. She would never entertain such an intimate gesture if she didn't have a connection with the man. Personal connection was not quite an accurate description of their association. During his vice presidency, Clarissa had discovered, quite by accident, that Nelson had certain proclivities. Working late one evening, she had walked into his office to find him with his pants down around his ankles and him vigorously rutting one of the interns from behind. She would never forget the look of horror and surprise on both their faces at her appearance.

Ever the opportunist, Clarissa knew she could use the situation to her advantage. Without batting an eyelid, showing neither shock nor anger at the carnal display, she had locked the door, stripped off her clothes, and moved quickly to join them.

"It is a hard call to make, Richard." She leaned forward and placed her lips next to his ear. "But it must be made."

He nodded slowly as her touch eased the tension in his body. "Yes, I'll do it."

Clarissa straightened up and began to move away. Nelson's hand shot out and grabbed her forearm. "Stay."

"I will, but first we need to call the others back in to get everything ready."

He came to his feet, turned his body to face her, and pressed himself against her slim frame. His hand grasped a butt cheek and drew her closer. He reached up and ran his hand through her black hair while looking into her brown eyes. "Let them wait. I want you now. I need you to help me relax before we put the world at war."

Clarissa could feel the turgid mass pressing against her through his pants. She smiled. "Who am I to deny the President what he wants?"

It was at that moment she knew there would be no stopping the plans of the Cabal.

The screens in front of Clarissa Rhodes came to life, and her counterparts from across the globe appeared in front of her. "What is so urgent that it can't wait, Ares?" Aphrodite asked impatiently.

"You all need to prepare. Tomorrow our time, the President will announce that the United States is moving troops into Ukraine to face the Russian aggression."

"But there are no troops in Ukraine," Hades pointed out.

"There are now," Clarissa told him. "Or so the President thinks. Once the Russians see that there is a build-up of troops on their doorstep, they will be compelled to respond. You all need to make certain that your countries come to the party when asked for support."

"What has brought this on before we are fully

prepared?" Hades asked.

"We *are* prepared," Clarissa snapped. "Once things are moving, I will convince the president to send a force into Romania to secure their oil fields. Once that is achieved, we can start proceedings on the newly discovered field."

"Isn't it risky to start a war with Russia just to get at Romania's latest discovery?" Apollo asked.

"We all knew that this day would come," Clarissa told them. "We were going to have to go to war with the Soviets sooner or later. This way, we get paid to do it."

"I heard you lost one of your lieutenants, Ares," Athena commented. "Is it true?"

Clarissa bit back her anger. "Yes, Solomon Harris. Such a tragedy."

"How did he die?"

"What does it matter?"

"I was told he was executed by the man you framed for the assassination of your President. Have you found him yet?"

How I'd like to come through that screen and wipe that smug look off your Italian bitch face. "We are working on it. At the moment, we have more important things to address."

"You know we can replace you in a heartbeat, just as we did your predecessor," Adonis commented. "You might lead, but together, we have all the power."

"I am well aware of that," Clarissa snapped.

"Then let's hope your plan has fruitful results. You'll get your support. Just pray that it all works out."

The screens went blank, leaving Clarissa sitting there contemplating in silence. Her eyes narrowed as she felt red-hot fury build inside her. She tilted her head back and let it out.

CHAPTER 10

Ukraine, Eight Days Later

They were men of the Second Squad, Second Platoon, B Company of the 2nd Battalion, 503rd Infantry Regiment, 173rd Airborne Brigade Combat Team. Eight men in all under the command of a sergeant named McGregor. All were veterans of Afghanistan, and until recently, they had been stationed in Italy. Now they were on patrol along the border to Eastern Ukraine.

It was early in the afternoon and the sun was still high in the sky, an orange fireball burning bright above the forested landscape.

"Hey, Sarge, what the hell are we doing out here? There's no one around."

Without needing to turn around, McGregor knew who the griper was. "Can it, Parelli. We're two klicks from the front line, so shut the fuck up."

The patrol was a regular happening. HQ sent one out every four hours, as regular as clockwork. There had been no contact made since the commencement of the patrols three days before.

The deployment had been whirlwind. Orders had come down the pipe, and within a few hours, they were in the air. Headquarters and elements of the Engineer Battalion were stationed near Kiro-vohrad, where, along with the Support Battalion, they were setting up Camp Reagan, which would become the base for all American forces in-country. The rest of the battalions would be taking up their respective positions to the south, while the Second Cavalry had come from Germany and were now in position in the north.

Suddenly the radio crackled to life, *"Bravo One... heavy...I say..."*

"Bravo One, this is Bravo Two. Say again your last, over," McGregor said into his radio.

"Mac, this is Grunter. We're taking heavy ground fire. We walked into a fucking ambush."

"Where are you, Grunt?"

He came back and giving him the grid reference. McGregor looked at his map. "Grunt, we're about two klicks from your position. Hold on, we're coming."

"Copy, Mac. You'd better hurry. This is fucked up."

"Did you send for fast air, Grunt?"

"Can't raise them. I'm surprised we got you."

"I'll see what I can do," he replied. Then, "Break. Bravo Alpha, Bravo Alpha, Bravo Alpha, this is Bravo Two, copy?"

"Read you Lima Charlie, Bravo Two."

"Bravo Alpha, we have TIC, troops in contact, at this grid reference." He gave them the numbers and continued, "Bravo One is requesting fast air. I say again, Bravo One is requesting fast air ASAP, over."

"Roger, Bravo One. Fast air is on the way."

Another voice came over the radio. "Mac, is that you?"

It was the battalion's commanding officer, Colonel Radford Holland. "Yes, sir."

"What's the situation, son?"

"Grunt has been ambushed, sir. We've called in fast air for him, and we're going to make for his position. He's two klicks from us."

"Why isn't he calling it in?"

"His signal is screwed up, sir."

"All right, Mac. Get on it, son."

"Yes, sir."

McGregor turned to his men. "Let's go, men. Bravo One is in trouble. Move."

Over Ukraine

"Viper Two, this is Viper Lead. Drop to one thousand, and we'll see if we can wake these guys up."

"Roger that, dropping to one thousand."

"You still with me back there, Slammer?" pilot Griff "Crater" Hutchins asked his weapons system officer Benjamin Wallace.

"I'm still here, Crater," he replied.

Hutchins took the F-15E Strike Eagle down to one thousand feet and started his run at seven hundred knots along the valley where there were troops in contact and asking for help. "See if you can raise our troubled friends, Slammer."

"Bravo One, this is Viper Lead, do you copy, over?"

There was no response, so Wallace tried again. "Bravo One, this is Viper Lead, do you copy, over?"

Nothing.

"I can't raise them, Crater."

By the time the transmissions ended, the F-15 had blown out the other end of the heavily treed valley. "Hang on, Slammer, we're going around. Viper Two, we're going around again. Can't raise ground troops at this time. Drop to five hundred, and we'll see if we can get visual."

"Roger, Viper Lead, dropping to five hundred."

The passage of the planes echoed throughout the valley as they traversed it once again. "Keep an eye out for ground to air, Slammer. We're close to the border here."

Both planes carried out another pass without positive results. "Slammer, try them again."

"Bravo One, this is Viper Lead. Do you read, over?"

Silence.

"Bravo One, this is Viper Lead, over."

Hutchins sighed into his mask. "What was that other callsign they gave us?"

"Bravo Two. It was another patrol."

"Try them."

"Roger that," Wallace replied. "Bravo Two, this is Viper Lead. Do you copy, over?"

"Roger Viper Lead, this is Bravo Two. Read you Lima Charlie, over."

"Yeah, Bravo Two. We're trying to raise Bravo One, and we can't seem to get through."

"Copy that. We're about one klick to the north of their last confirmed position. We can hear gunfire, but we haven't been able to raise them either."

"Understood, Bravo One. There's not much we can do if we don't know their location, over."

"How about a zoom and boom, Viper Lead?"

"Wait one, Bravo Two," Wallace replied. "Crater, Bravo Two is requesting a show of force over the last known area of Bravo One."

"Roger, Slammer. While we're here, we might as well burn some fuel."

"Bravo Two, that's an affirmative on the show of force."

"Thanks, Viper Lead. Bravo Two out."

"Viper Two, this is Viper Lead. Bring them around and drop to one hundred. Show of force required."

"Copy, Viper Lead. Viper Two coming around for a show of force. Dropping to one hundred."

The show of force required no firing of weapons, just a high-speed pass at low altitude, breaking through the sound barrier at just the right time so the sonic boom exploded deafeningly over the enemy's head.

Hutchins eased the throttle on the F-15 forward, and the plane's Pratt & Whitney F100-PW-220 afterburning turbofans responded. He was thrust back into his seat as the pure power took over.

Then it happened. Everything turned to shit.

"Crater, I've got an alarm. We're being painted. Looks like...yep, we've got a Grumble."

"Grumble" was the NATO callsign for the SA-10 Surface to Air Missile system utilized by the Russians.

"Where?"

"It's on our...wait, they've got lock. Firing. Shit, Crater! Launching decoys. Break right, Crater. Pull up now."

The F-15 turned almost violently, inflicting powerful G-forces on those inside. A missile streaked between the two planes, passing through the air where Viper Lead had just been.

"Eagle Nest, this is Viper Lead. We've been fired upon by unknown forces with an SA-10. Request permission to engage."

"Roger, Viper Lead, you're cleared to engage."

"Viper Two, did you see where that came from?"

"Roger, Crater. Our friend is just about to—"

"Missile, inbound. Break left! Break—"

The orange fireball in the sky was tinged with black as the F-15E of Viper Two exploded with the impact of the SA-10. Burning debris began raining over the ground beneath it.

"Fuck, Crater, they got Swivel. Jesus!"

"Pipe down, Slammer. Find that damned missile launcher."

"Shit, we've got another missile in the air. Launching decoys—"

"Motherfu—" Hutchins saw this one coming; it had been launched ten degrees off the right side of the plane. The white contrail pinpointed the launcher. The *second* launcher.

"Two, we've got two separate launchers, Crater." Slammer's voice exploded in his ears as Hutchins put the F-15 into another evasive maneuver.

In a calm voice, Hutchins said into his radio, "Eagle Nest, this is Viper Lead. Viper Two is down. I say again, Viper Two is down. No chutes visible at this time."

"Copy, Viper Lead. We're launching Viper Three and Four. They're five minutes out, over."

"Three! We've got three missile launchers, Crater. This is a fucking ambush."

"Viper Lead, do you read, over?"

"Where is it, Slammer?" Hutchins asked, ignoring the radio call.

Wallace read him the coordinates. "That's on our side of the damned border, Slammer. Get it right. Look again."

"I know it is, Crater, but it's there, damn it."

"Eagle Nest—"

"Missile launch port side, Crater. Break right, break right."

"Launch decoys, Slammer."

"We're out."

"Shit, hang on."

Hutchins pushed the throttle lever all the way forward and the afterburners kicked in. He rolled right and then climbed left. "Where is it, Slammer?"

"Coming up on our six, Crater," the weapons officer said in desperation.

"Tell me when, Slammer."

"Wait…wait…wait…break left! Break left!"

The Strike Eagle rolled left and the missile streaked past the plane, narrowly missing it. "Jesus Christ, Crater, that was close. Let's get the hell out of here."

"I'm with you," Hutchins said. He turned the Strike Eagle and pointed it to the west.

"Viper Lead, this is Bravo Two, over."

"Reading you, Bravo Two."

"Are you guys all right? We saw what looked to be a missile launch."

"It was a trap, Bravo Two. Your boys were the bait. It cost me a wingman."

"Shit, sorry about that."

"Not your fault. Just see if you can find the one on your side of the fence. You do, holler, and we'll come back and stuff his day up."

"You're telling me there's a SAM site on this side of the fence?"

"Roger that."

"Damn it. What do we do meantime about Bravo One?"

"Didn't you hear me? It was a trap. Your friends are dead. We've got two more Strike Eagles on the way from base, but you need to find that SA-10 launch site. Give me your position, and I'll have my weapons officer point you in the right direction. We're bingo fuel and need to land."

"Roger that, Viper Lead. Good luck."

"You too, Bravo Two."

"Bravo Two, this is Slammer. Prepare for coordinates of the SA-10 site."

"Send, Slammer."

The sound of the F-15E Strike Eagle melted into the distance, and for the first time in a while, McGregor realized he couldn't hear gunfire. He turned to his second in command. "Chuck, over here."

Corporal Chuck Rivera hurried over to his sergeant. "What is it, Mac?"

"We're deviating from our track," McGregor said. He took out his map and showed Chuck the coordinates. "The fast air said there's an SA-10 site here. We need to find it for them to take it out."

"A missile launcher on this side of the fence?" Rivera asked disbelievingly.

"Yeah. Get the others ready."

"Wait, Mac, what about Bravo One team?"

"We have to assume they're lost, Chuck. That was a trap to bring in fast air, and it worked. They shot one of them down. Listen, try to reach them while I radio our change to Bravo Alpha."

"Roger that."

"Bravo Alpha, this is Bravo Two, over."

"Roger, Bravo Two. Read you Lima Charlie, over."

"Bravo Alpha, Bravo Two has a change of mission, over."

"What's going on, Mac?"

"If you don't know already, the whole thing was a trap to lure fast air in and take them down with mobile SA-10 launchers."

"We were monitoring the outcome."

McGregor said, "One of those is on this side of the fence. The pilot of the surviving bird gave us coordinates to check."

"What about the other patrol, Mac?" This time it was Holland.

The sergeant looked at Chuck, who shook his head. "Sir, the firing from their location has ceased, and we can't raise them by radio."

"That doesn't mean they're all gone, Sergeant."

"Yes, sir, but we'll need medivacs if we find survivors, and we can't do that with a missile launcher on our side of the wire."

"All right, Mac, continue on your new mission. I'll have A company out in the field within twenty minutes."

"Roger, sir. Bravo Two out."

"All right, Chuck, get them moving. You're on point."

"Why me?" the soldier asked.

"Because apart from me, you're the only one I trust to get the job done."

"I found it," Chuck said in a hushed whisper as he sank down beside McGregor. "It's about one hundred meters ahead of us."

"Russians or militia?" the sergeant asked.

"I don't know?"

McGregor's stare hardened. "What do you mean, you don't frigging know?"

"I couldn't see anyone."

The sergeant frowned. "What?"

"There was no one there. If there was, I couldn't

see them."

"Shit, stay here with the others. If I need you, I'll use the radio."

"You watch yourself, Mac."

"I'll be right back."

McGregor gripped his M4 tightly and quietly began making his way through the trees. It took several minutes, but the launcher soon became visible in a small clearing. The massive vehicle sat in silent contemplation, its launch tubes pointed skyward, waiting for its next meal. McGregor crouched and swept the area in front of him, looking for any sign of life.

There was no movement whatsoever around the launcher. As he scanned farther afield, beyond the vehicle, McGregor missed it the first time, but as he returned on that vector, he spotted it—the lump on the ground in olive green. "Shit," he hissed in a low tone.

He got to his feet and moved slowly out of the trees into the clearing where the launcher was sited. He crept forward, sweeping left and right with his M4.

When he reached the lump, he found a man in camouflage, shot in the head. He frowned. *What the hell is going on?*

The sergeant started walking around the launcher and found more dead men. "This isn't right," McGregor muttered to himself.

The sergeant pressed the talk button on his radio.

"Chuck, bring them up. You gotta see this."

2nd Battalion, 503rd Infantry Regiment, HQ, Ukraine

"There was something off about it, sir," McGregor told Holland. "They were dead long before that Strike Eagle was brought down."

"Well, who was it then, Sergeant? Ghosts?"

"I'm telling you, sir, they didn't shoot down the plane."

Holland turned away and stared across the hive of activity that was their camp. He caught sight of the full body bags being loaded into the waiting Black Hawk and stood looking that way for at least thirty seconds before turning back. "Tell me again what you saw."

"They, I mean the battery crew, had all been shot in the head. They were stiff, sir, with rigor. Besides that, there was one other thing that made me suspect they were staged."

"What's that?"

"A boot print."

"A boot print, Mac? That instills no end of confidence in me."

"It was an American boot print, Colonel."

Holland hesitated, thought, then said, "What do you want to do, Mac?"

"I want to go back out and see what I can find, sir."

"All right. Take two squads, go out tomorrow, and look around. Three-day patrol if you need it."

"Yes, sir."

"Watch your ass, Mac."

CHAPTER 11

Outside of Jackson, Wyoming

...resulting in the ambush of a flight of two F-15E Strike Eagles by Russian missile forces. Reports are that one of the American planes were shot down with no survivors. American ground troops confronted the threat and attacked the Russian troops on Ukraine soil, neutralizing them all. The message from the White House is that US and NATO troops will not treat this act of aggression lightly, and adequate responses are being discussed.

Meanwhile, sources in Russia deny that all Russian forces were on the Ukraine side of the border and state that any missiles fired at the American aggressors came from the Russian side.

The Russian president has said that if NATO keeps up its aggressive stand against the Motherland, it will have no choice but to react. The area is seeing a build-

up of troops from both sides.

Hank Jones switched off the television in disgust and dropped the remote on the small table beside his chair. "What a lot of damned horseshit," he growled.

"That's about all you find on the television these days," said the old man sitting in the chair beside him. "Never watch it myself. Too much to do wrangling horses and nursing cows."

Jones turned to him. He wore a long-sleeved cotton shirt and jeans tucked into riding boots. "Jim," he said, "sometimes I think you're better off."

"Since my boy's been gone, I occasionally watch it to see if the world has broke. Looking at this, I'd say it's missing a sizable chunk."

What remained of the team had made their way to Wyoming, going to ground until the time was right to resurface. The place they'd chosen was the ranch belonging to Anvil's father. On their arrival, the old man had recognized Jones right away. He'd said to them, "If I thought for one minute you all were bad, I'd get my gun and shoot you myself. But when you showed up here, you had one thing going for you: my son. I trust his word more than anything in this world."

"He's a good soldier, Jim," Jones agreed with a nod.

"No, sir. Matt's more than that. He's a good man."

They sat there in companionable silence, then Jim asked, "How are you all going to dig yourselves out o' this mire, General? You're the most wanted man in America at this very minute. That applies to the others and my boy too. If I'm honest, and no offense, I don't give two figs about you or them, but my boy is everything to me."

Jones nodded. "I understand, Jim. No offense taken. Truthfully, I'm trying to figure it all out but getting nowhere really fast. I'd rather be back in Vietnam any day than trying to deal with this shit. At least over there, you knew who the enemy was. At the moment, it is hard to know who to trust."

"You was a grunt?" Jim asked him, raising an eyebrow and looking at him with a renewed sense of respect.

"75th Rangers, running recon."

"Military Assistance Command Vietnam Studies and Observations Group," Jim replied.

"No shit," Jones said, his impression of the man rising even further. Recon was dangerous work. MACV SOG, that was a whole other notch above.

"You can stay here as long as you need to, General, but remember, they're going to show up here eventually."

Jones nodded. "I've thought about that, and the last thing I want is to bring the war to your doorstep."

"Might be able to fix that. Five klicks west of here, I have a cabin the cowboys use sometimes. It ain't much, but it might do for the five of you."

"All right. If it helps keep you out of it, then we'll do that."

"I'll send the cook into Jackson for supplies. You'll not be able to take a vehicle up that far so we can hide it elsewhere. You ever ride a horse?"

Jones smiled and shook his head. "Do I look like I ever *rid* a horse?"

"Nope. Most likely, you only ever rid a Huey with a horse painted on it," Jim said. "Is there anything you need in town?"

"I'm sure I can think of something."

Washington, DC

The phone rang, and Rear-Admiral Alexander Joseph picked it up. "Joseph."

"Hey, Boomer. We scrambled?"

"Like a dozen dropped eggs on a concrete floor," Joseph replied. "It's good to hear your voice, my friend."

"It's good to hear yours, Joe. I'm sorry about your boys."

"That's war, General. How are the others?"

"They're good."

"You heard from Reaper?" Joseph asked.

"Not a word," Jones replied. "Have you picked up any scuttlebutt?"

"Your boy is causing all kinds of chaos, Hank.

He got out of Syria and got the others out of the fix they were in. Now they've dropped off the face of the earth."

"Well, you can expect him to surface sometime, Alex. When he does, there's going to be hell to pay."

"Speaking of paying, I heard Solomon Harris has gone to the boneyard."

"Asshole pissed me off. He deserved what he got."

"Damn, Hank, ain't you a little old to be going black?" Joseph asked, tongue in cheek.

"What happened to put us on a damned war-footing with the Russians?" Jones asked.

"Word was that the Russians were gathering forces along the Ukraine border."

"Word or intel?" Jones asked.

"CIA intel," Joseph said mockingly. "It smacks of Cabal. I reached out to a friend at the DIA, and they told me that there was no Russian build-up before the President started funneling troops into the country. Now it's a damned race to see who can get the most there first."

"But why induce a war with Russia?" Jones asked out loud.

"Give you one guess. Romania's oil."

"There's not enough to warrant a damned shooting war, Alex."

"They found a shitload underground a couple of months ago," Joseph told him.

"A new field?"

"Yeah, bigger than anything in Europe at the moment."

"Has Nelson ordered troops down there yet?" Jones asked.

"No. It's been suggested, though."

"How did the security council let this happen?"

"It wasn't them. Only a few people met with the president before this shit went down. Paul Brewer was one, and the new chairman of the joint chiefs was the other."

"Your friend, does he have any evidence about the fake build-up?"

"Yes."

"Can you get it?"

"I have it, Hank."

"I want you to send it to Jackson, Wyoming. Have someone hand-deliver it to…wait…" There was a drawn-out silence before Jones said, "The Shady Rest Coffee House. Send someone that will be known on sight."

"Surely you're not coming to get it, Hank," Joseph said, bemused.

"Just send it."

"All right, it'll be there by oh-nine-hundred to-morrow."

"Thanks, Boomer."

"Stay safe, Hank."

The call disconnected, and the rear-admiral turned in his chair. He thought for a moment about

who he could send, then he turned back to his desk
to make the call.

Brewer entered Clarissa's office and waited for her
to motion toward the seat in front of her desk. "Do
we have a problem, Paul? It's about the only time I
get to see you these days. The Ukraine thing went
well, but I'm guessing that is about to change."

"It could be a good problem, ma'am."

"How about you tell me and let me be the judge
of that?"

"I had Alex Joseph's office tapped amongst other
things…" He saw her mouth open and held up a hand
to ward off her protest. "Don't worry, it won't be
found. CIA, remember?"

"It had better not be."

Brewer ignored the comment and carried on.
"Anyway, our friend received a call from the general—"

"Jones?'

"Yes."

"Where is he?"

"I'm getting to that. Anyway, their discussion
went on for a while, and eventually it came around
to the little fracas in Europe. It seems that Joseph
has a friend at the DIA who came across intel that
could prove our pictures and such were faked."

Clarissa stared at Brewer through granite eyes. "I

hope you plan on taking care of this person?"

"Just as soon as I find out who it is," he replied. "However, Joseph has the proof on him and is sending it to Jones, who requested it."

"Where?"

"Jackson, Wyoming."

"You need to intercept it before it reaches him, and then find the old bastard and finish this once and for all."

"I was thinking maybe we could follow the fox to the henhouse."

"Then get him and the evidence?"

"Yes, ma'am. And the admiral?"

"Leave him. If Jones slips away from us, he still might be useful. After we get Jones, then and only then will we deal with Rear Admiral Alex Joseph."

———————

Ukraine

"Chuck, over here," McGregor said as he looked around.

"The bodies are gone!" Chuck exclaimed.

The sergeant nodded. "Yeah."

The launcher, or what was left of it, was wrecked from an airstrike that had been called in.

"Maybe the airstrike did for them," Chuck proposed.

"No, they were taken away. Set up a perimeter."

Chuck started to bark orders while another sergeant, a big man a full head taller than McGregor, approached. "What are we doing, Mac?"

Sergeant Charlie Cross was in charge of 3rd squad. He, like McGregor, had seen service in Iraq and Afghanistan.

"I want to have a look around here before we move on. You got anyone who thinks he's a tracker?"

"I have someone. Young fire-breather who thinks he's Kit Carson."

"Now's his chance to prove it."

Over the next thirty minutes, they waited while the young airborne trooper looked around, studying everything with his intense gaze. McGregor and Cross watched his movements. McGregor said, "He looks like he knows what he's doing."

"Likes to think he does."

When he was finished, the young soldier walked over to them and said, "The dead were taken away by ten or so men."

"Which way did they go?"

"Southwest."

"All right, do you think you can follow them?" McGregor asked.

"In my sleep, Sarge. There is one thing, though."

"What's that?"

"Whoever they were, they weren't Russian unless they took to wearing US-issue boots."

"Well, soldier, you find those men wearing US-is-sue boots. Lead out, you're on point."

"Yes, Sergeant."

The young man turned away, but Cross stopped him. "Wait, I'll walk it with you. That way, some-body will be watching for trouble all the time."

McGregor watched them walk off and pressed the talk button on his radio. "Chuck, get them to-gether. We're leaving."

"Mac, hold up. We've got something." Cross' voice wasn't much more than a whisper as it came through the radio.

"Roger," he replied. Then, "Chuck, we're stopping here. Post a rear guard."

"Copy, Mac."

McGregor turned to the man behind him and said, "Wait here."

He then started forward through the trees. They'd been following the trail for about a klick. He found Cross and the young soldier he'd learned was called Waters approximately two hundred meters farther on.

"What is it?"

Cross pointed at the ground in front of him, and McGregor saw what had pulled them up: freshly dug and covered-over graves. "Looks like someone doesn't want anything laying around out in the open."

"Why hump them a mile and then bury them?" Waters asked. "It doesn't make sense."

"It does if you've got something to hide," Cross said to him. "You want to dig them up and have a look, Mac?"

"Just one. We'll take a picture and cover him back up."

The task took twenty minutes. The soldier they uncovered was, as expected, wearing a Russian uniform. He also had been shot in the head. McGregor didn't bother to search his pockets; he didn't need to. That had been done when they found the missile launcher and came up empty.

"It is like they were all executed," McGregor told Cross.

"But why? Ukrainian troops, you think?"

"If it was, we'd have known about it. Someone on their side would have said. No, this is all kinds of weird."

McGregor called the kid over. "Where did they go?"

"They kept heading southwest."

"All right, let's follow."

McGregor hugged the dirt as bullets cut through

the air no more than a few inches above him. The smell of rotting vegetation and blood filled his nose. He stared into the open, sightless eyes of Chuck Cross, who'd taken two rounds in the opening volley. They'd walked into an ambush so devastating that eight of the sixteen-man patrol had fallen immediately.

That included the kid and Cross, who'd borne the full blast of a claymore.

All around him, McGregor could hear the shouts of scared and troubled men. Some were wounded, others just wanted to get the hell out of the fire zone.

The sergeant tried his radio again. "Eagle Nest, Eagle Nest, this is Bravo Two, do you read me? Over."

"Bravo Two, this is Eagle Nest, over."

"Eagle Nest, this is Bravo Two. We are currently taking heavy fire. Over."

"Roger, Bravo Three. What's your status? Over."

"Bravo Three is KIA. I have many casualties, my position. We are pinned down."

"Can you disengage, Bravo Two?"

"Neg—" A bullet plowed into the dirt near him and made McGregor flinch. "Negative, Eagle Nest."

"Mac, you hear me?" Holland asked.

"Affirmative, sir."

"You dig the hell in, soldier. We're coming for you. Birds are spinning up as we speak. Give us your position, son."

"Yes, sir." McGregor rattled off the coordinates.

"We'll be there soon."

"Roger that. Bravo Two, out."

The gunfire grew heavier, as though the ambushers realized their time was running out. McGregor looked around his position and saw the carnage. Then he saw the depression to his right. In it were two of his squad. He took a deep breath and started crawling toward them, bullets burning the air above him and burrowing into the ground all around.

With one last lunge, he rolled into the depression. One of the soldiers looked around and saw who it was. "This is fucked up, Sarge," he said anxiously.

"Just keep shooting, Peters. Help is on the way."

McGregor pressed his talk button on his radio. "This is Bravo Two to all callsigns. Fall back on me. I repeat, fall back on me. Acknowledge."

He received three replies. They came in through a hailstorm of gunfire that was chewing at their heels. One was a corporal from Cross' squad. "Mac, they're all around us."

"Tell me something I don't know, Gracey."

Grace looked around the depression and asked, "Where's Cross?"

"He's gone."

"Shit."

"Just keep firing."

McGregor fired in desperation, trying to keep his remaining few alive. Then came a troubling a call from one of the soldiers to his left. "I'm down to one mag, Sarge."

"Me too," said another.

McGregor pressed his talk button. "Eagle Nest, this—" He stopped.

"Gracey, on me," he shouted to the corporal.

Grace slid over to him. "What?"

"Whoever is out there can hear our transmissions. I've got a plan."

"I'm all ears."

A few minutes later, Corporal Allan Grace said into his radio, "Bravo Two, this is Charlie One, over."

"Read you, Charlie One, over," McGregor replied.

"Bravo Two, we're about three mikes out from your position. We'll be coming in from the northwest, over."

"I hope you brought plenty of help, Charlie One."

"We brought the whole company, Bravo One."

"Charlie One, we're taking heavy fire from all sides. Suggest you split your force and try to flank."

"Roger that, Bravo Two. Sounds like a plan. Will radio when in position."

"Copy, Charlie One. Bravo Two out."

As suddenly as the firefight had begun, it ceased. McGregor looked at Grace. "I think they bought it, Gracey."

"You were right, Mac."

"Check the wounded and stay off the radio. We need them to think help is almost here. If they have any inkling that we pulled a fast one, they'll be back, and we can't stand another attack."

"Roger that."

The final tally was eight KIA and two WIA. The rest had somehow escaped unharmed.

CHAPTER 12

Jackson, Wyoming

A battered pickup truck sat across the street from the coffee house as the two men inside it waited patiently for their contact to appear. Hunt sat in the passenger side with his hand tucked under his coat, gripping his sidearm should it be required in a hurry.

Next to him, Striker said, "I don't see why we have to wear these frigging cowboy hats. A ballcap would have done."

"Stop complaining. You look like John Wayne or Joel McCrea."

"Who?"

"Shit, Striker, you really need an education."

"I'm damn well educated enough."

Hunt looked at his watch. It was nine-thirty, and he was beginning to think that the courier wasn't going to show. "We'll give it until ten and then get out of here," he said to Striker.

A further ten minutes elapsed in silence before they saw a Lincoln Town car pull up outside the intended meeting point. They watched a middle-aged man unfold himself from the rear of the vehicle, stretching the kinks from his spine. "Shit," Striker said. "Is that who I think it is?"

"Looks like it."

"I thought he'd be dead by now."

"Don't much look like it," Hunt said as the man disappeared into the coffeehouse. "Come on, let's go say hello."

"He'll probably find a puddle to make us lay in somewhere," Striker theorized.

"I guess we'll find out."

They climbed out of the truck and crossed the street, looking both ways but seeing no traffic on the sleepy town's road. The sidewalk outside was swept and clean, and as they pushed through the coffee house door, the heavenly aromas of roasted coffee beans, biscuits, cake, and other kinds of food hit them in the face, making them salivate. They looked around the crowded room for their man and saw that he was sitting toward the rear of the café, giving his order to a waitress. She nodded and walked away, leaving the man by himself.

"Come on," Hunt said and started toward the table.

As they arrived, the man looked up and said,

"Shit, if I'd have known it was you, I'd have brought life preservers for the pair of you."

They sat down and said, "Good to see you too, Senior Chief."

Senior Chief Grady Ruggles had been their BUDS instructor when they had tried out for SEALs. He was as tough and as salty as they came, and though neither would admit it to the man, he was the reason they'd made it through.

"I hear you ladies have yourselves in a bit of a jam," he growled as he rubbed his stubbled jaw.

"Still fighting, Senior Chief," Striker said.

"As you damn well should be," he snapped in a low voice. "I wouldn't expect anything else from my boys."

The senior chief reached into his coat, took out a letter-size envelope, and slid it across the table. "Take this. I hope it's what you need."

"Thanks, Chief," Hunt said, taking it and tucking it inside his shirt.

"You boys should know that I think I was followed here," Ruggles said grimly.

"You sure?" Hunt asked.

"Trust me. There're two suits over your shoulder, just sitting there. They came in not long after you did. Personally, I would have waited for you to emerge, but these guys seem overly aggressive. CIA would be my guess."

"And where there're two, there are more," Striker growled.

"I'm sorry, boys."

"You'd better come with us, Senior," Hunt said. "Forget going home for a while."

"You mean, come with you two and get shot at and chased by bad guys, maybe even killed?"

Striker nodded. "Something like that."

"I'm in. Lead the way."

"Wait here," Hunt said and climbed to his feet.

Ruggles frowned. "What is he up to?"

Striker grinned. "He's going to say hello."

Ruggles watched as Hunt as he strolled casually toward the door. As he drew level with the men, he grasped a handful of hair on the man who was facing away from him with his left hand and slammed his face into the table hard. Blood spurted, and the man went limp.

While this happened, Hunt's right hand swept around, filled with his H&K45C. He pressed it into the chest of the second man so there would be no mistake, no chance of a customer being hit by a stray bullet, and pulled the trigger.

The report, though muffled, was still loud and brought forth exclamations and cries of alarm from most of the customers, few as they were.

"That'll work," Ruggles said out loud.

"Time to go, Senior," Striker snapped.

They got up and followed Hunt, who'd resumed his casual stroll toward the door. A man fumbled with something under his coat, and a handgun appeared. Striker pulled his and pressed it against the nape of the man's neck. "Didn't your mama ever tell you it was dangerous to play with guns?"

The man froze, and Ruggles took the weapon from his hand. He dropped the magazine out of it, ejected the round from the breach, disconnected the slide, and threw it on the table.

They made their way out with no further problems and stood on the concrete sidewalk. Hunt was already walking away from them to the left. Striker called after him, "That ain't the way, Scimitar."

"Yeah, well, fuck the way," he snapped.

Striker frowned and wondered where the hell he was going when he saw the two black SUVs lined up at the edge of the gutter. "Shit."

He dug into his pants pocket and pulled out the truck keys, then tossed them to Ruggles. "The truck across the street, Senior Chief."

Ruggles caught them and started across the asphalt.

Behind him, he heard Striker say, "This is a bad idea."

———————

Hunt knew what they were as soon as he saw them, and being pissed wasn't helping his thinking any. The blatant assassination of the man in the coffeehouse was out of character for the SEAL, but he'd had all he was going to take from the damned Cabal. As he strode toward the two black SUVs, he knew just what he was going to do.

When he was close enough, the H&K came up, and he fired at the first vehicle. The front window spider-webbed as holes appeared in it. The two men sitting in the front lurched violently as rounds punched into their bodies. The passenger doors flew open, and two more men tumbled from their seats. Both were armed with M4s and were trying to get them into action.

Hunt fired at the first of the two and put him down with three rounds. He cursed under his breath when he realized his slide was locked back. His magazine was dry and he dropped it as he reached for a fresh one to insert. The dreaded feeling of knowing he was going to be too late washed over him.

A weapon barked beside him as Striker opened fire at the second shooter. The man collapsed to the ground and writhed in pain. "You need to get a grip, Bord. That was stupid."

Hunt nodded as he let the slide of his weapon go back into place, taking a round with it into the chamber. "Yeah, but right at this moment, I don't give a shit."

They advanced toward the second SUV, and as they did so, it backed up at speed with a screech of tires. Both men opened fire at it and saw their bullets hit home.

The SUV did a reverse-handbrake turn, and the

nose of it spun a hundred and eighty degrees before the driver stomped on the gas and it sped away.

Their truck pulled up beside them. "Come on, Bord, it's time to go."

They hurried toward the truck. Striker opened the passenger door and Ruggles said, "Get me one of those carbines."

"What?"

"Get me a fucking carbine, Striker. Your damned ears painted on or what?"

Striker scooped up one of the M4s and looked quickly for spare magazines. He found a couple and climbed into the truck beside Hunt. After all these years, things hadn't changed. Ruggles was already scolding Hunt for being reckless.

"Just frigging drive," Hunt growled.

"Don't you speak to me like that, damn it. You were wrong, and you know it."

"All right, now shut up and drive before we end up in even more shit."

Ruggles stomped on the gas and the truck shot forward with a deep roar, leaving chaos in its wake.

Washington, DC

"I didn't send you to Jackson to turn the place into a damned war zone," Brewer growled into the phone.

"That wasn't us," White said. "One of them just went off the rails and killed one of our people. That was before the shit went down outside."

"What were two officers doing inside in the first place?"

"We needed eyes in there. Standard practice. You and I both know that," White said. "The problem now is that with the county sheriff stomping around looking for them, it'll make things harder."

"I might have something there. One of the SEALs has an old man out there near Jackson. If I were to guess, I'd say that is where they're hiding."

"What, a ranch?"

"The perfect place to hide."

"Send the coordinates, and I'll deploy there. Ask the old man a few questions."

"Whatever it takes. This has gone on for too long. And one more thing: try not to lose any more men. It's becoming a damned habit."

2nd Battalion, 503rd Infantry Regiment, HQ, Ukraine

After receiving McGregor's report, Holland picked up his satellite phone and dialed a number from memory. A voice on the other end said, "This better be damned good."

"Alex, it's Rad Holland. I hope I'm not interrupting anything, sir."

"Good to hear your voice, Rad. What's up?"

"I need your help."

Joseph was about to say something when he stopped, thought, and said, "I've just got something to do, Rad. Can I call you back?"

"Sure."

"All right. I'll talk soon."

It wasn't even five minutes before Joseph called him back on a separate encrypted satellite phone. "Sorry about that, Rad, but the walls have ears."

"You got troubles?"

"Like you wouldn't believe. What's up?"

Holland told him of the events of the past few days, and Joseph slowly digested it. Then in a grim voice, he said, "What I'm about to tell you, Rad, could get us both in a lot of trouble, maybe even killed. If you still want my help, then I'm all in."

Holland didn't even hesitate. "Lay it out for me, Boomer."

Outside Jackson, Wyoming

"This can't be good," Jim said as he leaned on the two-pronged fork he'd been using for hay.

The SUV bounced along the narrow dirt road that led up to the ranch house, leaving a long trail of dust rising in the sky behind it. It swung into the yard and stopped. Four men climbed out of the vehicle, but only one walked forward. The others, all armed, stayed with the SUV.

"Are you Mister Thomas?" White asked, smiling at the rancher.

It was easy to see there was nothing but coldness to it. Jim nodded. "I am."

"I'm looking for your son."

"He ain't here."

"You sure about that?"

"I said so, didn't I?"

White nodded slowly. "I think you're lying. I think you know where he is."

Jim's eyes narrowed. "Get the hell off my land, Mister, before I have my hands throw you off it."

White's smile broadened. "Is that your last word?"

"Yes, sir. It is."

"Shame."

Seemingly from nowhere, White produced a handgun and shot Jim in the chest. The old man fell back and lay spread-eagle on the hard-packed earth of the ranch yard. The CIA specialist turned to his men and waved at them. They rushed forward to start their search, and gunfire soon began to ring out.

Ten minutes later, it ceased. One of the men came over to White. "They're not here. If they were, they would have shown by now."

"Then we need to make them show themselves."

"How are we going to do that?"

White looked at the body on the ground. "I have an idea. Burn everything."

———————

From the cabin, they saw the rising smoke as it painted the sky dark brown farther along the valley. Jones, Striker, Hunt, and Ruggles had been inside looking over the intel supplied by Alex Joseph. Beforehand, Jones had called Joseph and told him in a roundabout way that he was compromised. Then he'd proceeded to chastise Hunt for going off the reservation. He was halfway through that when Rucker came inside and told them about the smoke.

"It's the ranch," said Anvil.

Jones looked at the SEAL and noted a certain edginess about him. "Gear up," Jones said. "Let's go and take a look."

They climbed into the vehicles and drove away from the cabin, Hunt and Jones in the truck while the others followed them. Hunt said, "Do you think they followed us from town?"

"Not likely, Chief. I'd say they found out through looking into our backgrounds."

They pulled up in a stand of tall pines about half a mile from the ranch house. After climbing out of the vehicles, they walked to the tree line.

As they looked out from the rise they were on,

they could see the burning buildings. Everything in the ranch yard was on fire. Anvil gasped and took a step forward before he was grabbed by Striker. "Hold up, kid."

"I gotta get down there. My pa—"

"We'll go, Matt," Hunt said to him. "Striker and I. You stay here."

"Chief—"

"Your ears painted on, son?" Ruggles demanded. "You take orders when they're given. Do you understand?"

Anvil stared defiantly at the older SEAL, but Ruggles was having none of it. "Do you understand?"

"Yes, Master Chief."

"Good. You stay here with me and the doc. If this is a trap, we still have the mission to carry out."

Hunt checked his ammunition and adjusted his body armor. Beside him, Striker did the same, and once completed, they began the walk toward the ranch.

They could feel the heat, even though there was still around fifty meters to traverse to reach the yard. Hunt's sweep pattern was from twelve o'clock to the right while Striker swept to the left. "We have a body just ahead, Striker."

"Roger that," the SEAL replied.

Hunt checked the fallen man. It was one of the hands; he was dead, shot in the back as he was trying to get away. "He's gone," Hunt said. "Moving."

"Hey, Bord, I was just thinking that if we saw this smoke, the other hands will have too. They'll be making hard for here."

"Yeah, that's why we have to secure this thing as soon as possible."

The two SEALs entered the yard and stopped suddenly. "Mother of God," Hunt whispered.

Striker moved to stand beside him. "This is fucked up, Bord."

Bodies were strewn everywhere, left to lay where they had fallen. Hunt counted seven. However, one hadn't been left to lay. It had been hung from a tree in the yard. "Son of a bitch," Hunt growled as he walked toward the strung-up rancher.

They stood before him, looking up as the corpse slowly twisted in the breeze. A note had been pinned to his chest with a knife. Hunt reached up and tore off the blood-stained piece of paper. It said:

This is what happens when you interfere with things that don't concern you. Give him up and we'll go away. You'll find us in Jackson at the Clover Leaf Motel. Come tonight or not at all. Remember this: we are unlike anything you've dealt with before. There is nowhere you can run or hide. We are the Cabal, the new world order. Mr. White will be waiting.

Hunt passed it to Striker, who read it. Hunt

pressed the button on his radio. "Rucker, bring them down. We're secure here."

"On our way."

"Striker, help me get the old man down before Anvil gets here."

It took them the rest of the day to inter the dead. They all stood around the old man's grave, staring at the mound of damp earth covering it. Jones stared at Anvil. "I give you my solemn promise, Matt, that every one of them will get the burial they deserve once this is all over."

"This is my fault, General," he said somberly. "I was the one who brought us all here."

"That's horseshit, son, and don't you forget it. The responsibility for all this lies squarely at the feet of the Cabal, and trust me, they'll pay for it."

"How?"

"Striker and I will go to the motel tonight," Hunt said.

"Not without me, you're not," Ruggles said. "I'm up for it."

"Me too," Anvil said.

Striker shook his head. "You and Rucker stay to keep an eye on the general. It is more than likely a trap."

Over Ukraine

A C-17 had been rerouted for a special mission. Onboard was a four-man team of SEALs, the result of a phone conversation between Holland and Alex Joseph. Each man was well prepared with extra ammunition, a couple of Black Hornets, and small Nano UAVs that were easy to hump around the combat zone.

They were only minutes out from their jump and would HALO in. Their commander was dark-haired Senior Chief Nick Dawson, a veteran of the teams who'd seen action in Africa, Afghanistan, Syria, and the Philippines. With him was his second in command, Ben Tyler. Then there were Tank Brown and Daisy Philips.

Daisy had come into his name during an op where he'd landed in a flower garden after a parachute malfunction. His reserve had deployed, but by then, he was way off-course and landed in a patch of rose bushes, which turned out to be nasty. As he was getting patched up, he'd moaned, "Why couldn't it have been fucking daisies?"

Hence the name.

The mission had come from the man himself, Rear Admiral Alex Joseph. His instructions for the op were clear, and then he'd signed off. Soon after that, alternate orders had come through an encrypted source. Their DZ had changed by one thousand meters, and their jump time had changed by ten minutes. Dawson had thought it strange until he was told the real purpose of his mission.

The whir of the lowering rear ramp interrupted his thoughts. Signaling his men, they rose as one and began shuffling toward their jump point. In the distance through the dark, the SEALs could see flashes rippling with concussive blasts—the reason for the change in their DZ.

Three Boeing B-52 Stratofortresses were dropping their payloads over the area, part of a plan cooked up between Holland and Joseph. The latter had deliberately laid a trail of misinformation in his office for those he knew were listening, but that had all been altered.

The jump light changed color, and the SEALs shuffled off the ramp and fell into the abyss.

———

Dawn found the SEALs amid a moonscape of bomb craters and trees smashed to kindling. In the middle of it somewhere was the drop zone the SEALs had originally been told they were going to use.

They found the first body lying at the bottom of a crater, not a whole body but most of one. Dawson turned to his man. "Spread out."

The SEALs started searching for any more signs. There were bits and pieces everywhere, but it was Tank who hit the jackpot. "Hey, Skywalker, east side of the bombing zone."

"On my way."

Dawson made his way over to where Tank stood at the edge of the trees. Lying at his feet, curled up into a ball, was a man. He was shaking, mumbling, bloody, and wide-eyed.

"I think he's seen better days, but if you give me a little rope, I might be able to get something out of him. Bombs stuffed him up real bad."

Dawson shook his head. "Get him ready to travel. I'll radio for a chopper."

"What are Americans doing waiting for us out here, man? This is all kinds of fucked up."

Dawson nodded. "Yeah. Get him ready."

———————

Washington, DC

Clarissa looked at the screens before her and could tell that some of the others were less than pleased with the progress in Ukraine. "What is holding everything up?" Athena asked in her usually abrupt tone.

"The President is waiting for more troops to arrive before he makes his next move," Clarissa responded. "I thought having the planes shot down would be enough, but it wasn't."

"You need to persuade him to send troops into Romania. You have men in the area. Send them into Romania and start blowing the wells."

"I wish it was that simple."

"What do you mean?" asked Hades.

"We lost contact with them a few hours ago."

"How did you lose contact with them?" Hades sneered.

"Let me see. How about I fly over your home with a B-52 and drop bombs on it and work out if we remain in contact?"

There was silence.

Clarissa continued. "Have you found the others yet, Hades?"

"No."

"Then don't start lecturing me about how things are going. Overall, they're going fine."

She cut the feed to the screens before she went on a rant that there would be no coming back from. She looked at Brewer. "Tell me about Mister White."

"He's reasonably sure he'll have Jones tonight. Let's just say the message he left will be impossible to ignore."

"I hope you're right, Paul, because that old bastard is starting to royally piss me off."

Jackson, Wyoming

"How many?" Hunt asked Striker.

"I found two outliers to the east and another to the north."

Hunt nodded. "Yeah, the same to the south and west. I figure there's a couple in the SUV, and our man White is in room seven."

They had arrived an hour after dark and staked the motel out while they watched and waited. When they thought the time was right, they walked the perimeter. Now they had a fair idea of what they were up against.

"What do you want to do, Bord?" Striker asked.

"Whichever way we decide to do it, it'll have to be fast. I was going to suggest we take out the two in the SUV, then take out White. But if they get off an alarm, they could trap us inside."

"So we tidy up the perimeter first," Striker said. "Work from the outside in."

Hunt looked at the senior chief. "You ain't said nothing since we arrived."

"Just admiring the way you boys work."

"You reckon you're up to taking down a few roving Joes?"

"On my worst day," Ruggles boasted.

Hunt nodded. "Let me know when you're all in position."

They climbed out of the SUV and went their separate ways. Five minutes later, the call from both outriders came over the comms. "In position."

Hunt took a deep breath and said in a low voice, "Execute, execute."

———

Inside room seven was White, seated at the small square table where his handgun lay waiting for action. He had seen a thousand just like it in his travels for his job, one drab motel room blurring into another.

His team, or what remained of it, was spread out around the motel, intending to close in when the others arrived. However, he also knew not to underestimate his quarry since they were smart and very well trained, so he'd posted a second quick response team a block away in a black SUV—four armed men who specialized it tough jobs.

White was on edge. He'd never come across a target such as this before. Normally, the mission would have been put to bed by now, but these were something special, and it made him feel rueful that he had to kill them all.

When he looked at his watch, it told him it was a little after nine. He sighed, wishing this was all over and he could return home. He hated waiting.

When the sound of gunshots came, he knew it

was time.

He picked up the handgun from the table and waited for what was to come.

The door flew back, crashing against the wall, and a figure filled the doorway. White fired four times.

———————

As soon as he drew level with the SUV the CIA operatives were in, Hunt opened the passenger door and fired twice across the closer man into the driver. He cried out and slumped across the wheel, bleeding onto the floor mat.

Although he was on high alert, the sudden and unexpected violence stunned the second operative and his reaction was slow, giving Hunt the time required to subdue him. He clipped the man with his H&K, stunning him while he relieved him of his weapon. Then he grasped a fistful of coat and dragged him from the vehicle.

"Stand up, asshole," Hunt cursed as the man staggered, trying to get his legs beneath him. In seconds he righted himself, but Hunt was already pushing him toward the motel room door.

Upon reaching it, Hunt kicked the door hard. As it flew back, he stepped behind the CIA operative, using him as a shield. Four bullets hammered into the man, and Hunt felt every one of them. He let the dying man fall and fired at the figure standing in the center of the motel room.

Hunt heard the man inside grunt, then he saw him buckle at the knees. The SEAL stepped over the body he'd dumped in the doorway and entered the room, keeping his weapon on the man on the floor. "You White?"

The man looked up at Hunt through pain-filled eyes, giving him a wry smile as blood spilled from the corner of his mouth. His attempted chuckle came out as more of a grunt. "Y-you guys are good, I'll...give you that."

"You screwed up going after the kid's old man."

"Wasn't after...him. Was looking for...Jones."

"Who sent you?" Hunt asked. "Was it Brewer?"

"Who do you reckon?"

Hunt nodded. "Yeah, it was him."

There was movement behind him, and the others joined him, Ruggles remaining in the doorway. Striker said, "We need to get out of here, Bord."

"In a moment." He stared at White, watching him die.

White looked up at him and gave him another wry smile. His breathing got shallower until his chest was hardly moving, then he died.

Hunt checked his pockets.

"Damn it," Ruggles growled. "We don't have time for this shit."

Hunt ignored him and found what he was after: a phone. It was locked, but he knew how to bypass that. He quickly scanned for numbers. "A number" was a better description. After all, there was only one, repeated ten or so times. Hunt dialed it and waited.

It clicked on the other end, and a voice said, "Is it done?"

"Your man is dead, Brewer," Hunt said, guessing who was on the other end.

"Who is this?"

"You know who it is."

There was a sigh. "Yes, I guess I do."

"Well, know this too. We're coming for you. It might not be immediately, but it'll be soon, and when you least expect it. Understand? Real soon. And when we do, there'll be no coming back from it."

Hunt hung up and said to Ruggles, "Now we can go."

They hurried across the lot and into their vehicle. As they pulled away, another SUV with the four CIA quick response men in it appeared. They were too late to help anyone.

CHAPTER 13

Falkenburg, Austria

Falkenburg was a castle in the Austrian Alps. Surrounded by giant gray slabs of snow-capped peaks, it sat in a long, lush green valley dotted with pines. It looked like a scene out of a big-budget medieval movie, only it was real.

On one of the battlements, Kane stood gazing across the valley, wondering what it was like back in the day, seeing an advancing army coming to attack or lay siege to the castle.

"MI6 certainly know how to do a safehouse," Cara said as she walked up behind him.

Kane turned and smiled at her. "If only things were different," he said to her.

"What, you'd bring me here for a holiday, Reaper?" she joked.

"Why not?"

Cara stood beside him, placing her hands on one of the solid crenellations. She sighed. "It's taking far too long to find her, Reaper. I'm really worried that we won't, or if we do, it will be too late."

He nodded. "Between Swift and MI6, I was hoping they'd have found something by now."

With all that had been happening, certain elements of MI6 had been brilliant about providing assistance to the team. It made a difference that Knocker knew people from when he'd been running missions for them.

The man behind their escape from Turkey and responsible for their current residence was an MI6 officer named Noah Bancroft. He and his hand-picked team had gone off-book and were working with the WDI to try to stop what was quickly becoming a global disaster.

When Kane and Ferrero had first explained their problem, they'd expected the MI6 man to be full of scorn, but Bancroft was only too willing to help, already being suspicious of the Cabal and their global network. The list was just icing on the cake.

Besides, he was more than certain MI6 had its own Cabal moles.

It was Brick who brought them the news while they stood taking in the vista. His boots on the flagstones heralded his approach. They turned and saw the excitement on his face. "We found her, Reaper. She's in Hong Kong."

———————

"What do we have, Luis?" Kane asked as they entered the large, high-ceilinged room being utilized as their ops center, with computers, tech gear, and big screens spread across the space.

"Show him, Slick," Ferrero directed.

The rest of them had also gotten word and were gathering as well. The large screen showed the front façade and circular driveway of a large building. "This is the Hong Kong Princess," Swift told them. "Don't ask me how we did it because I don't have the time nor the inclination to tell you. Just be satisfied that we have found the general."

The screen changed, showing a picture of five people standing near a vehicle at night in the drive of the hotel. Four of them were men, and the fifth was a woman. The picture zoomed in on the woman and became quite grainy, but with a few simple keystrokes of Slick's magic fingers, it cleared up. "That there is the general."

And it was.

"Who is she with?" Kane asked.

"The results of the search I performed on these guys came back a little disturbing." The screen changed again, and an Asian man's face appeared. He was middle-aged and looked mean. "This is Hong Liao, or as they say in China, Liao Hong. He, ladies and gents, is the boss—"

"Of the Hong Kong Triad," Kane finished. "He's the guy we tried to shut down in the US."

"That's him. I take it that you also know the guy on his left?"

"Zou Lin, his right-hand man. I see he's still alive. Obviously that bullet Cara put in him didn't slow him down much, and it certainly didn't kill him."

"Should have put one in his damned head. Would have helped the world."

"How long ago was this?" Kane asked.

"About eight days ago. Liao has a whole floor to himself on the…let me see."

The picture changed to a full shot.

"Fucking hell, mate," Knocker burst out. "Please tell me he don't live on the top floor of that thing."

"No, only on the seventy-second. His people are on the seventy-first."

"How tall is it?"

"Eighty-four."

"That," Knocker growled, pointing at the screen, "is fucking bollocks right there."

"Why do you say that?" Ferrero asked.

"There's no way you can get up to that floor without being seen, which means the only other way is come down from the roof. Since that part of Hong Kong has restricted airspace, the only way to do it is to fucking parachute onto it. There's but two people able to hit that size of target with only a ten percent chance of succeeding, and that's only if they're frigging crazy enough to try it."

They all looked at the SAS man. "Are you saying you're one of them?" Axe asked.

"Yeah, I am. No offense to you Recon guys, but how long since you did a HAHO jump onto a dime?"

"Who is the other?"

"He means me," Brick said, taking a step forward. "Trying to hit that thing will be as bad as it gets. I know you can all jump, but you're not qualified for this. I'm not doubting your courage because I know you would all try it. Hell, even we might end up splattered on the sidewalk for the street sweepers."

Kane looked at them. "So, are you volunteering for the jump?"

They simultaneously answered, "No."

Kane gave them a curious look and Knocker said, "But we'll go anyway. Because if we don't, one of you will try to do it, and I'm not waiting down the bottom to wipe you up with bog roll."

Axe opened his mouth. "Toilet paper, Axe, effing toilet paper," Knocker snapped. "Remind me to buy you a British dictionary when this is over."

"I was just going to ask if you wanted to be buried in a jam tin or a peanut butter jar."

"Can we get back to the briefing now?" Swift asked.

"You have more good news?" Knocker asked.

"It gets better."

"Do tell."

"There are guards on the roof."

Knocker's face took on a look of exasperation. "Of course, there are. Next, you'll tell me he owns… You know what, don't bother. We'll just shoot them as we come down."

He looked at Brick, who nodded. "That'll work."

"If we zoom in here," Swift continued as the screen flicked over, "we'll see an external elevator shaft. It is Liao's."

Kane's eyes followed it all the way to the roof. "Is that the only access to his floor?"

"Apart from the internal stairwell, yes."

"What if there's a fire in the building?" Teller asked.

"It will be an express train."

"A what?"

"The elevator is rigged to detach from the cable. Once it does, it'll go into freefall until it gets almost to the bottom, where the automatic brakes will come on."

"That won't stop it from going splat," Axe pointed out.

"The shaft extends below the surface for what equates to another three levels. Once down, it will open, and whoever is inside can exit along a tunnel away from the building."

"So, the only way to get to the floor where Liao is holed up is to use his elevator or the stairwell?"

Kane asked for clarification.

"Yes."

Knocker and Brick stared at the building in the picture, each knowing what the other was thinking. "Well?" Brick asked.

"I guess," Knocker replied.

Ferrero frowned. "What are you two thinking?"

"We'll need a door opener," Brick began.

"That would be good," Knocker agreed.

"Are you going to explain or keep talking in braille?" Kane asked.

"Providing we get to the roof without dying along the way," Knocker continued.

"We'll rope down to the floor," Brick finished.

"Except we'll need Cara to help us get in," Knocker added.

"How? You want me to use my boobs again?" Cara asked.

They all laughed, then Brick said, "No, nothing like that. We'll need you on the building across the way with a long gun."

"A Barrett M82 should be good enough," Knocker explained. "You shoot out the window just before we hit it."

"You want me to blow out a window with a fifty-caliber sniper rifle?" Cara asked.

Knocker grinned. "Yes, but don't worry too much about it. We'll probably be dead by then."

Kane nodded. "OK, say you get that far. You'll

have people at the bottom waiting for you."

The Brit shrugged. "We'll take the express car."

"You'll cut the cable and—"

"Ride that bitch all the way down, yeah," Knocker finished with a smile.

"Ballsy move," Traynor remarked.

"Riding the express like that, balls is right," Cara said. "You'll be wearing them for earrings by the time you stop."

Kane said, "You'll still need cover when you get to the bottom."

"You got someone in mind?"

"I know a chap."

The Brit grinned. "I'll bet you do."

Arenas looked at Swift. "Can we run the operation from here?"

The computer tech nodded. "I can try."

"Make it happen, *amigo*. For the moment, we're safe here. No sense in all of us going to Hong Kong and walking into the lion's den."

"I'll do my best, Carlos."

The Mexican turned to Kane. "We need to get confirmation that the general is still there. No sense going all that way and finding nothing."

Kane turned to Bancroft, and the MI6 man nodded. "We should be able to confirm that."

"Thanks, Noah."

"I'll be able to get you in and out of Hong Kong within twenty-four hours."

"You're a legend."

"You know, best of British and all that. Pip-pip."

"All right," Ferrero said. "Make plans, people. Carlos, once you and the team work out something, bring it to me."

"Yes, sir."

"Let's get the general back, people."

———————

The Hong Kong Princess, Hong Kong

Thurston was hurting. She'd been tied to the steel chair for eighteen hours a day for the past eight days, or was it nine? Shit, it could be frigging ten, she thought. All she knew was that it hurt like hell and she'd had enough.

The room in which she was being kept was like a steel box. No windows for light, and a mattress in the corner for the few hours of sleep she was permitted. In the right rear corner of the room was a camera recording her every move, its little blinking red light taunting her day and night. Not that she could tell the difference. Everything was starting to blur.

Since her arrival, Thurston had been trying to figure out why Liao was keeping her alive instead of killing her. Once she'd even asked him, but the smug bastard had smiled coldly at her and said nothing.

To keep her mind off her situation, she often found herself thinking about the others, wondering if Ferrero and the rest of Bravo were still in the Turkish prison, or if they were even still alive. Then there was Reaper and his team. She knew that should they have made it out of Syria, nothing short of a damned division would stop them coming for her or the others, but what they were fighting was worse than any division. The insidious Cabal had infiltrated every corner of the globe.

The door opened, interrupting her thoughts. Liao appeared with Zou. "Good morning, General Thurston," the triad boss hissed. His tongue flickered as he licked his lips, making him look like the snake he was.

"Is it?" Thurston asked. "Is today the day you finally kill me? If it is, then let's get it the hell over with, asshole."

Liao chuckled. "No. Today I have something special for you."

"Really? You brought me ice cream? You're so fucking generous, Liao. How about a bath? I smell like shit."

The man ignored her. "Today, you will have a visitor."

Thurston stared at him. She wanted to fire something back at him, but her curiosity got the better of her. "Who?"

"Someone from the mainland. From the Ministry of State Security."

"Wow, things are getting serious," she responded, trying not to show her sudden nervousness.

"He will be with us for several days, so you should be quite well acquainted by the time he's finished."

"When do I have the pleasure of meeting him?" Thurston asked.

Liao smiled knowingly. "Funny you should ask that. He's already here."

It was obviously the cue the man was waiting for because he suddenly appeared in the doorway: a short, unassuming man with a solemn-looking face. Even his eyes looked sad. He said in a quiet voice, "Good morning, General Thurston. My name is Hou. I look forward to getting to know you."

"Bite me, asshole."

CHAPTER 14

Hong Kong

Bancroft was true to his word. He'd had the team in Hong Kong within twenty-four hours of confirming Thurston was still alive in the building, and now they were counting down the final minutes to their operation. Even though Hong Kong had reverted to Chinese rule, the British still had a solid presence behind the scenes.

Kane and Axe were in a black Range Rover a block away from the target building. They were decked out in their tactical gear and were armed with all their weapons. Kane pressed the talk button for his comms. "Reaper Two? Reaper One. Confirm in position, over."

"Copy, Reaper One. Reaper Two is in position."

"Bravo Four, copy?"

"Copy, Reaper One. Read you Lima Charlie, over."

"How are we looking?"

"I'm hooked into a satellite, Reaper One. It's the best I could do, over."

"Roger," Kane replied. He looked at Axe. "At least we're going in only partially blind."

"I don't care if Knocker does get under my skin, Reaper. He and Brick have my respect on this one. They miss, and they're all kinds of fucked up."

"Shut up, Axe."

"I mean, could you imagine scraping them up—"

"Shut up, Axe."

"—all squishy—"

"Axe!"

Axe pulled a spatula from out of nowhere. "Good thing I brought this."

Kane shook his head and laughed. "You're a dick, you know that?"

"Yeah, but I'm all yours."

"Shit, now I'm going to have to shoot you."

Kane looked at his watch. Two minutes to jump time. *Let's hope they don't miss.*

Over Hong Kong

Knocker and Brick gave each other the thumbs-up. Knocker checked the GPS on his forearm and waited for the ramp of the C-130 to finish lowering. They would jump from twenty-seven-thousand feet in a

HAHO, which was High Altitude, High Opening, and then glide thirty kilometers to their target.

Wearing oxygen masks and goggles, they shuffled forward, attached leg bags holding the extra equipment they needed. They stood at the edge of the ramp, bumped fists, and fell into oblivion.

Fifteen Seconds After Leaving the Plane

The parachute opened without any problems. Knocker felt the comforting jerk as it deployed, and then he reached up. He looked around and saw Brick off to his left a hundred or so meters and said into his comms, "You OK, Brickster?"

"That was the easy part," Brick replied.

"Isn't that the truth."

Knocker patted his chest to make sure the suppressed H&K 416 was still there. He and Brick had discussed the landing, and there was no way around it. There was no way to take out the guards on the rooftop before they landed, not if they wanted to live.

He saw the ex-SEAL adjusting his flight path, so he checked his GPS and did the same.

The pair frequently checked their altitude and GPS. The lights of Hong Kong glimmered on the horizon as they sped toward them.

"This is going to be dicey," Knocker muttered to himself.

The Hong Kong Princess, Hong Kong

Black parachutes backdropped by a night sky. Even if the guards had looked up, there was every chance they would not have seen them. Knocker worked his risers as the building in front of him grew quickly.

He suddenly realized he was cutting it fine. Actually, it was more than fine; there was a good chance he was going to come up short. He had two options—bail out and turn away, or keep going and possibly leave a Knocker-sized imprint on the side of the building. Whichever choice he made, it had to be now.

"Hell, Knocker, nothing wrong with leaving your mark on the world."

Right up until his boots touched the edge of the rooftop, Knocker was seriously doubting whether he would make it. It wasn't until they did that he knew he was safe. Kind of.

A gust of wind filled the parachute before it was collapsed and began dragging the SAS man across the rooftop.

"Oh, bollocks," he blurted as he started to skid along on his back.

That, however, was not his only problem. That award went to the guard who'd spotted him and was bringing his MAC-11 machine pistol up to cut loose.

Knocker grabbed his suppressed 416 and wrenched it around. As soon as it settled on the would-be shooter, he squeezed the trigger and the weapon ripped out a long burst of fire, punching holes in the triad guard. The man collapsed to the rooftop and dropped his weapon with a clatter.

With the threat neutralized, Knocker could concentrate on the problem at hand: stopping his careening rush toward the edge of the building.

He tried to unlatch the quick-release harness, but nothing happened. "Come on, you cock," he growled, hitting the buckle.

The SAS man saw the edge of the rooftop rushing toward him. The parachute canopy was already over the lip, and he was about to follow it when a rail loomed in front of his NVGs. Knocker grasped at it desperately and made the catch with his right hand.

A shout reached his ears as a second guard saw him and pointed his MAC-11 at the Brit. "This is not sodding happening," Knocker growled and was about to do the only thing he could and let go when the flat report of a suppressed weapon sounded.

The second guard collapsed without firing a shot, then a hand firmly gripped his arm and a voice said, "You done fooling around?"

"Just help me out, will you?"

Brick helped him get his parachute under control. Once done, he said to Knocker, "You better let them know we're down safe."

"I always wanted to do this," the Brit said with a smile. "Reaper One from Reaper Three. The eagle has landed. I say again, the eagle has landed."

Brick shook his head with an audible snort. "You're a dick."

"Copy, Reaper Three."

"We're moving to phase two. Reaper Two, stand by."

"Reaper Two, standing by."

They found anchor points for their ropes and tied them off. Then they adjusted their equipment, making sure it was all secure. Lastly, they tossed the ropes over the edge of the building and hooked on, ready to rappel down. Knocker looked over the edge and all the way down to the street below. For a solitary moment, vertigo gripped him, but he managed to thrust it aside and began his climb over the edge.

Brick said, "I hate heights."

"Me too," Knocker replied.

"Well, aren't we a great pair?"

"Do you think if our ropes snapped, we would be dead before we hit the ground?"

Brick smiled in the dull moonlight. "I want to know if it hurts when we hit the deck."

Knocker pressed his talk button. "Moving to phase three. Reaper Two, we're on our way."

"Roger that. Be aware we have two men in the room at point of entry."

"Copy that."

The two men started their perilous descent down the glass-filled face of the Hong Kong Princess.

———————

Cara used her binoculars to look up the side of the building Knocker and Brick were coming down. Then she settled back in behind the Barrett to wait for their call for her to do her part.

She looked through the scope at the two men in the room that was the point of entry. Both wore suits and were armed. They were just standing talking to each other. She adjusted the sights on top of the sniper rifle and centered the crosshairs on the triad man on the left. She took in a couple of deep breaths to ease her nerves, which were partially caused by knowing that two of her people were seventy-plus floors above a sudden death stop at the bottom. She'd heard of airmen falling from bombers at twenty thousand feet with failed parachutes or none at all and by some miracle surviving, but there was no way that should that happen here, they would do anything but die.

"Reaper Two, we're approaching next phase."

"Copy, Reaper Three. You're approaching next phase. Just say when."

"On my mark."

Cara aimed at one of the guards behind the glass.

"Three...two...one...*now.*"

Cara squeezed the trigger and the Barrett slammed back into her shoulder, its .50-caliber projectile on its way across the void.

The glass of the window shattered and collapsed, and the two assaulters swung in through the cavernous opening. Brick brought up his 416 and fired the weapon at the second guard, who stood stunned, having witnessed the head of the man he'd been talking to suddenly become pulp, spattering blood all over him.

Knocker and Brick detached themselves from the lines and started to sweep the apartment. A triad shooter appeared with a MAC-11, saw the two operators, and made to shoot them. Both Knocker and Brick burned him down with a burst of gunfire. The issue was that the dying man had his finger on the trigger and sprayed half a magazine of bullets into the floor before it fell from his lifeless hand.

They moved left, sweeping the kitchen, then hurried to the main bedroom, which they found empty. They were about to try the next one when three armed men appeared, the first of which was Liao. The second one was his henchman Zou, and the last one they didn't know.

Knocker shot Zou in the head with a well-placed

shot as Brick took out the third man with two in the chest. Liao tried to shoot Knocker with the gun in his fist but was too hasty. The bullet flew wide, missing by a good distance. The Brit shook his head and shot the triad boss in the leg. The man cried out in pain and fell to the floor beside his dead troubleshooter.

Knocker hurried over to the fallen man and looked down at his pain-filled face. "Hello, old cock. That leg of yours looks like it hurts."

"I'll kill you for this," Liao hissed.

"Yeah, whatever. Where is she?"

The triad boss said nothing.

"Where is she?"

Nothing.

"Brick, keep an eye on this guy, will you?"

"I'll put a bullet in him if you like," Brick replied.

"Might be an idea."

Knocker went toward the room from which the three men had emerged. It was a bedroom, nothing large but—it was too small. The Brit ran his eyes over the walls and furniture before he saw it. There were bookshelves against the far wall, but they didn't touch the floor. They cleared it by about half an inch.

"Let's see what this is all about."

He walked across to the bookshelves and pulled on them, and they came away on one side to reveal a doorway behind them.

Knocker stepped through and saw the figure

slumped forward on a chair in the middle of the room. "Shit," he hissed and lurched forward.

Thurston had been knocked around rather well. One eye was almost closed, and there was both fresh and dried blood on her face and other abrasions and bruises.

Knocker pressed the talk button on his comms. "Brick, second room. Get in here."

The Brit knelt in front of Thurston and looked up at her. "General?"

Her head moved slightly.

"General, it's me, Knocker."

Her good eye opened and focused on him.

He asked in a hushed voice, "What did the bastards do to you?"

She cracked a painful smile with swollen lips. "Where the hell have you been?"

Brick appeared, took one look at Thurston, and said, "Jesus Christ, what did they do to her?"

"Check her out. Make it quick."

"I've got nothing to help her with," the SEAL told him.

Knocker's head bobbed. "Just make sure we won't kill her if we move her."

As the SAS man walked out of the room, he pressed his talk button again. "Reaper One? Reaper Three. Jackpot, I say again, Jackpot."

"How is she, Reaper Three?" Kane asked.

"She's been knocked around some, Reaper.

Reaper Five is checking her out to make sure she is ambulatory."

"Roger that. Just so you know, we've got movement down here. I think they know you're there."

"I'm not surprised. Some dobber burned through half a magazine from his MAC-11. Reaper Three, out."

Knocker hurried through the main part of the apartment to where Liao lay bleeding on the tile floor. The Brit ignored him as he walked past to the doorway to the stairwell. He opened the door and listened. They were coming. He could hear them.

He said into his comms. "Brick, finish up. We're about to have visitors."

"I'm not done, Knocker. I need another couple of minutes."

"I'll do what I can."

Knocker found a chair and used it to prop the door open, then stepped out onto the landing and leaned over the rail in time to see the first of the armed men appear. He brought the suppressed 416 up to his shoulder and fired twice at the lead man.

Two rounds punched into the triad member, and he fell back down the stairs. Knocker shifted his aim and took down a second goon.

At the sight of the second man falling dead on the stairs, the shooters below opened fire, wildly firing up the stairwell without aiming.

Knocker shrank back as ricochets cut through

the air, narrowly missing him. He cursed them and returned fire with only the intention of slowing them down. Bullets from the 416 hammered down into the stairwell.

"Knocker!" Brick called.

"Get her into the elevator," the Brit shouted while ducking another storm of bullets.

He leaned back over to fire, but this time two of the triad shooters were providing covering fire for four others coming up.

Knocker fired down but missed, scarring the concrete walls of the shaft. He ducked back and did a tactical reload. Once he was finished, he leaned back over the rail, and the sight before him made him nervous. Three shooters now provided cover, and at least eight more armed with automatic weapons were hurrying up the stairs.

"Brick, you there yet?"

"Any time you're ready, Knocker."

The SAS man fell back into the apartment and slammed the door, locking it behind him. He could see Brick in the elevator and Thurston seated on its floor, leaning against the thin wall. As he walked past the wounded Liao, the triad boss sneered. "I will find you. Then I will kill you—"

The 416 in Knocker's hand moved as the SAS man shot the triad boss twice. "Shut the fuck up."

Behind him, something crashed against the locked door. "Looks like your boys are here."

"Come on, Knocker."

"Reaper Three? Reaper Two. You and Reaper Five need to get out of there now. You're—"

The rest of the message was drowned out by the sound of a helicopter outside the shattered window. Knocker stared at it and shook his head. "Well, that's something we didn't bargain for."

CHAPTER 15

The Hong Kong Princess

The MH-6 Little Bird hovered for a moment before its minigun opened fire to devastating effect. 7.62 rounds began ripping the apartment to pieces. Knocker hit the deck as the room around him seemed to explode. The sofa, the walls, television, table, and almost everything else took bullets. The apartment began disintegrating around the SAS man. "Shit, shit, shit, shit," he growled as he covered his head with his arms as though it would protect him.

The door to the stairwell opened and triad shooters rushed headlong into the death zone, only to be ripped to shreds.

"Cara!" Knocker shouted into his comms. "I need a distraction."

"On the way."

She started firing at the helicopter with the .50

caliber Barrett. Round after round punched into the aircraft as it kept up a constant barrage of fire from its minigun, seemingly oblivious to the threat Cara's weapon posed to it.

That, however, didn't last long. One of the heavy-caliber rounds found a component vital to the helicopter staying aloft, and the machine coughed, belching smoke from its engine. The MH-6 fell out of the sky.

As soon as the firing stopped, Knocker was on his feet, running through the debris strewn throughout the apartment. Behind him, the triad shooters had regained their composure and were firing at the running man.

Bullet kicked up at the SAS man's heels and sliced through the air around him. "This just fucking keeps getting better."

The open doorway into the elevator loomed in front of him, and in an act of desperation, he dived forward and slid across the hard floor into the elevator, crashing into the wall next to Thurston's crumpled form. She looked at him with her good eye and said, "Can't you ever *not* get into trouble?"

"Not my fault, ma'am."

Brick closed the elevator door as a fresh fusillade hammered into it. He looked at his companions, and warned, "Hold onto something."

Then he hit the emergency button, and the world dropped out from beneath them.

———————

Kane felt the vibration when the helicopter hit the street and could hardly miss the orange fireball that shot into the night sky, created by exploding Avgas. "What was that?" he called over his comms.

"Nothing, just a helicopter hitting the street," Cara replied.

"A what?"

"You know, a thing that has rotors—"

"I know what a helicopter is. What happened to it?"

"It had a slight disagreement with a fifty-caliber freight train."

"Damn it," Kane cursed. "Bravo Four, how the hell did a helo get past you?"

"I said I was good, not perfect."

"Get out of there, Reaper Two."

"On my way."

Kane looked at Axe. "Roll out."

Axe started the Range Rover and slipped it into drive. He planted his foot on the gas pedal, and the V8 engine roared and shot the vehicle forward. He swung around the corner and slammed on the brakes. A pile of twisted, burning metal was blocking their path.

"Back up," Kane snapped.

Axe started to reverse when a large Humvee pulled in behind them, cutting off their escape route. "Shit, ambush," Kane growled.

Axe looked left and right, seeing nowhere to go. "We're boxed in, Reaper."

"Out," Kane snapped, grabbing his 416.

Behind them, four men climbed out of the Humvee, all armed with automatic weapons. Kane shot the one who alighted from the passenger seat before the man could even fire. Axe was a little slower getting out, having had to negotiate the steering wheel of the Range Rover. By the time he got his weapon to his shoulder, the other three attackers were firing.

Bullets peppered the Range Rover, punching through the quarter panels and windows. Glass sprayed both Kane and Axe as they took shelter behind the vehicle.

"Who the hell are these assholes, Reaper?" Axe shouted to his friend.

"Give you one guess," Kane replied. "Zero, we're up the proverbial creek here. I need to know if there are any more surprises we aren't aware of."

"Reaper One, this is Zero-One," Arenas replied. "We've got two more contacts closing on your position. Estimate to be a further eight shooters."

Kane fired a few rounds at the tangos before dropping back down and asking, "Any idea who they are?"

"Slick has been able to isolate comms chatter, and we think they're German special forces."

"That's just great. Stand by, Zero-One."

"What did he say?" Axe asked.

"He says we're fucked."

"Just the way I like it," Axe said as he took out a second shooter.

"Cara, where are you?"

"I'm just about on the street, Reaper."

"When you exit, come east. We're not going to make the rendezvous point."

"Copy."

"And watch out for tangos. We've got more inbound."

"Roger that."

"Reaper Three, sitrep, over."

Nothing.

A storm of bullets rattled the far side of the Range Rover. A bullet snapped close, and then came the screech of tires. Kane turned his head and saw a second Humvee pull up. Three men got out of this one, while a second appeared in the roof hatch with an H&K MG4. Kane took one look at it and knew they were in trouble. "Axe, they've got a SAW."

The machine gun opened fire and started burning through ammunition at a furious rate. Kane sank down behind the battered Range Rover's engine block. "Reaper Three, sitrep."

"Man, that was a rush," came the reply. It sounded as though Knocker had been drinking beer all night and had a ballistic hangover.

"Where are you, Reaper Three?"

"We've just gotten out of the elevator. I swear we blacked out on the way down, man."

"Listen up, Knocker. We're in heavy contact with approximately six bad guys, with another bunch of tangos in the wind somewhere."

"Those bastards got down here quick."

"No, these guys are German Special Forces. The Cabal has found us. Our ride is screwed, and we're going to need wheels to get out of here. You can bet the Hong Kong police aren't too far away either after that chopper came down."

"Leave it to me, Reaper," the Brit replied. "I'll have us out of here in a jiffy."

"I need it to be sooner."

"Done."

More bullets peppered the Range Rover, making it rock and shudder under the impacts. Kane looked at Axe. "Help is on the way, brother."

"It better be," Axe said. "I'm down to my last frigging mag."

———————

When Knocker and Brick, the latter carrying Thurston in his arms, emerged from the tunnel into the underground parking garage, the Brit held them up as he looked for something to steal. At that point anything would do, but the latest vehicles were all but impossible to hotwire. However, in times of desperate need, someone always seems to provide for the despairing, as happened this time around. Knocker's grin split his face from ear to ear, and he said, "Thank you very much."

———————

"I'm out, Reaper," Axe shouted to Kane.

Kane grabbed his second-to-last magazine and tossed it to his friend. "Make the most of it."

Axe loaded the fresh magazine into his 416 and flicked his selector to semi-auto. He had twenty rounds to inflict as much damage as he could upon the attackers.

"Reaper Two, copy?" Kane said into his comms.

"Copy, Reaper."

"What's your position?"

"Godmother is in the house, Reaper," she replied. The transmission was followed by a deep boom, and one of the attackers was picked up by the hand of God and flung to the ground.

"Eat that shit," Axe growled as he saw the other shooters take cover.

"Cara, can you get the machine gun?"

"On it."

Another boom, and the gun went silent.

"That's got them thinking, Reaper," Axe called to the leader.

Not for long. These guys were professionals and

had been under fire many times before. "I wish you would shut up," Kane shouted back above the din. Then, "Reaper Three, where are you?"

"Get ready, Reaper. We're on our way."

"Roger that. Break. Cara, join us."

"Copy. On my way."

It took a couple of minutes, but Cara appeared at their side. With her arrival, they were only waiting on the others.

"Damn it, Knocker—"

Suddenly, a long limousine appeared. Brick was standing in the sunroof, firing his weapon at the German Special Forces. The vehicle slipped between the sidewalk and the two Humvees, the side mirror coming off when it hit a storefront.

Knocker brought it to a halt where it was facing the burning helicopter. His window came down and he called, "Get in."

Kane, Cara, and Axe ran for the open door and leaped into the limo. "Where the hell did you get this?"

"Our mate Liao. He won't be needing it anymore. And the—" Bullets hammered into the elongated beast. "And the best part is, it's armored."

He stepped on the gas, and the limo shot forward. Kane's eyes widened at the direction he was taking. "You can't—"

There was a sickening crunch as the front of the limo plowed through the wreckage of the helicopter, bulldozing it to one side. "Did you say something, Reaper?"

"No. Not a word."

Kane looked around and saw Thurston. Cara was sitting beside her. He asked, "How you doing, General?"

"The next time you send your men to nearly kill me, I'm benching you," she growled thickly from between swollen lips.

"I thought you'd like that. Not my idea, however. Blame those two."

"Reaper," Cara said. "She's—"

"I'm fine, damn it."

Cara gave Kane a pleading look.

"You let us be the judge of that, ma'am. Right now, you just take it easy, and we'll get you out of here."

"Step on it, Knocker," Brick called. "Those guys are after us."

The limo picked up speed as Brick emptied a magazine at the pursuing Humvees. Bullets hammered the rear of the beast as Knocker tried to draw away from them. A cross street loomed up on their left and Knocker jammed on the brakes, turning the wheel as he did so. The rear of the limo slid around, and once its nose was pointed at the street, he stepped on the gas once more.

The limo responded immediately and shot forward. Up top, Brick had changed his magazine and opened fire once more.

Up ahead in the amber light of street lamps, Knocker could see where the side street crossed a main thoroughfare. The SAS man gritted his teeth, and instead of slowing, he accelerated and blew through the intersection like a madman.

"Hey, you guys," Brick called. "We just picked up a third Humvee."

Brick looked back as the first Humvee tried to do what the limo had just done, but it was t-boned by a sedan. The front of the sedan crumpled like an accordion, and the Humvee lifted onto two wheels before landing on its side.

"That's one less," Brick called.

Knocker looked in the remaining side mirror and saw the carnage behind him. "Two to go," he said to no one in particular.

Then he had an idea. "Cara, get up there with your rifle."

Cara nodded. If anything was going to slow them down, it might be the Barrett. She tugged at Brick, who popped his head back into the cabin of the vehicle. "What?"

"My turn," she said.

"Be my guest."

The street on the other side of the thoroughfare narrowed and became an alley only wide enough for one vehicle, but it was piled with trash, which made the passage of the limo tenuous. The thing hit a large crate pile and unbalanced Cara, who was about to take her first shot at the trailing Humvee. She grunted as her ribs caught the edge of the sunroof opening and gritted her teeth as pain shot through her side.

"Damn it!" she exclaimed and brought the Barrett up to her shoulder, the bipod braced on the roof. "Here goes nothing."

She squeezed the trigger, not really expecting to hit anything the way the limo was dancing around. The weapon crashed, and the butt slammed back into her shoulder. The round flew straighter than she expected and smashed through the lead Humvee's front windshield.

The Humvee swerved, smashing its side against the wall of the building to its right. Then the driver straightened it and kept on coming.

Cara settled down to take aim again, but before she could, the limo shot from the alley and Knocker turned hard left, causing the rear of the vehicle to slide around. So unexpected was the turn that the Barrett's bipod slid across the rooftop and she nearly lost it.

Cara regained her balance in time to see the first of the two remaining Humvees wheel around the corner. The main thoroughfare they were on was a little smoother than the alley, which afforded her a better shot.

As soon as she thought her aim was good, Cara fired again, the round smashing into the front of the Humvee. It must have struck some vital part of the vehicle because it stopped as though hit by a sledgehammer.

"That's another one down," Cara called, taking aim at the remaining pursuer. Bullets peppered the rear of the limo. Cara was forced to retreat into the cabin to avoid the fusillade, and she took several deep breaths before popping back out. This time, instead of sighting properly, she just pointed and loosed a round.

The Humvee swerved as the window blew in, and Cara thought she saw the passenger jerk under the impact.

The limo swerved violently as a small taxi pulled out in front of it. From inside, she heard Knocker shout, "Watch where the hell you're going, you useless frigging ass."

Once again, Cara's ribs took the brunt of the sudden maneuvering, and she winced as pain shot through the already bruised bones. "This guy drives like shit."

She sighted on the last Humvee as more bullets from the light machine gun fizzed and cracked around her. The Barrett crashed again, and this time the Humvee stopped dead.

Cara slumped into the limo, holding the rifle. "We're done here."

Kane nodded at her. "What took you so long?"

Cara flipped him the bird and looked at Thurston. She was slumped sideways against Brick, her good eye closed. Someone was going to pay for this in a big way.

_____

Washington, DC

"Liao is dead," Brewer told Clarissa. "Hong Kong was turned into a war zone by whoever did it, according to the news feeds."

"I'm guessing we know the ones responsible for it?"

"Yes. It was them. They grabbed Thurston and took out more of the German Special Forces who were sent after them."

"Do you know where they are now?"

"No. Someone has to be helping them. We've cut off every avenue they use that we know about."

"Another country's intelligence service?" Clarissa asked.

"Might well be."

"Find out who," she said abruptly.

"Doing my best—"

"Do it better. What about Jones?"

Brewer shook his head. "Nothing. The newsfeeds are running him day and night, but still nothing. It's like he vanished."

"And Joseph?"

"Nothing from him either. He's gone quiet. He obviously found out we were tracking his conversations."

"Is there *any* good news?" Clarissa asked impatiently.

"I've given the go-ahead for a team to take care of the Romanian problem. They will attack one of the smaller wells, and when news breaks, Winkler will go to Nelson and discuss sending people to guard the other wells. Nelson will undoubtedly want to send American troops, but Winkler will recommend operators from the private sector."

Clarissa frowned. "Who?"

"People from Bright Spark Solutions."

"Are they still around?" Clarissa asked curiously. "I thought once their fearless leader was gone, they would have gone away."

"Winkler saw their usefulness and decided they would come in handy."

"I see. When will it happen?"

"Within the next twenty-four hours. The people have been hand-picked for their ability to speak fluent Russian."

"Let's hope it works. That pussy Nelson is still screwing around on whether to do something about the plane that was shot down. I'm beginning to think I was wrong about him. If we can get the private contractors on the ground in Romania, that might ease some of the pressure from the other Cabal leaders until we can force the President's hand."

CHAPTER 16

Washington, DC

The encrypted satellite phone buzzed, and Joseph picked it up. "What have you got?"

"We got ourselves a canary, Boomer," Holland said. "And he's singing like you wouldn't believe."

"Can you get me what you have?" Joseph asked his friend.

"Sure, just tell me where and when."

Joseph told him what he wanted done and then hung up. Twenty minutes later, he had what Holland had sent him. It was a video file, so he pressed play to watch. The recording was of the interrogation of a man who looked to be more than a little shaken, during which he gave his name and what he'd been doing when he was picked up. The longer it went on, the closer to the edge of his seat Joseph got. At one point, he muttered, "Fucking asshole."

By the time it was over, Joseph knew what had happened with the attack on the planes over Ukraine, and by whose orders.

He looked at the clock on his wall, picked up his satellite phone once again, and dialed a number. A voice on the other end said, "Talk to me, Boomer."

"I have something you might be interested in."

"Is it good?"

"It's better than good. It might be what you need to start getting your life back."

"Well then, I guess I'd best take a look at it."

Outside of Jackson, Wyoming

After the attack on the ranch, the small group moved farther into the mountains to where Anvil's father had once had a cabin. "Ain't it strange for your old man to have a cabin back here when he had a ranch in a prime position?" Striker asked Anvil when they arrived.

"He used it to get away from my ma," the SEAL explained. "Sometimes when they fought, he'd come up here. I think a lot of it had to do with his experiences in Vietnam."

They'd decided to lay low for a while and see how things shook out. Two calls changed everything. The first was from Ferrero.

"We got her back, General."

"Damn good work, Luis," Jones said. "How is she?"

"She's been knocked around some. I'll know more when they get back."

"Rotten bastard. I hope they made him pay."

"I believe so, sir, but it wasn't Liao who did the worst. It was a Chinese security agent."

"Chinese?" Jones sounded surprised.

"Yes, sir."

"At least you got Mary back. What are your plans, Luis?"

"Well, sir, I'm thinking we've had about all that we can take from those assholes. Maybe we should scratch a few off the list. Show them they're not as untouchable as they think."

"Do you have any idea who?" Jones asked.

"Might as well go for the big fish, sir. I figure the better the job, the bigger the fish."

"Be careful. Do you need anything?"

"We've got a friend who's helping us out, sir."

"Understood, Luis."

"How about you, sir? Are you doing OK?"

Jones told him what had been happening while they'd been gone and about the intel Joseph had gotten to him.

"What do you plan on doing with it, sir?" Ferrero asked.

"I'm not sure yet."

"Good luck, General."

"You too, Luis."

The call finished, and Jones looked at Hunt. "They got Mary back."

"That's good news, General."

Jones nodded. "Yes, it is."

"They're also going after the Cabal over there."

"Payback?"

"Something along those lines."

Jones' phone buzzed. He picked it up and knew exactly who it would be. "Boomer?"

"I've got something special for you, Hank."

"The last time you gave me something special, Boomer, shit happened."

"You'll want to see this. Besides, I can have it to you a lot quicker. You got access to a computer?"

"I think the guys have a Toughbook somewhere."

"Get it and get back to me."

The call disconnected.

———

Hunt looked at Striker, who nodded. "I agree," was all he said.

Hank Jones shook his head. "These people think they're the ultimate patriots. They're damned murderers is what they are."

"What do we do with this, General?" Hunt asked.

"We use it. We need to get this guy back in the States and set up a meeting with the President."

"You think he'll meet with you, sir?" Striker asked.

"That depends on how good Boomer is."

"Boomer? Sir."

"Rear Admiral Joseph. He's the only one in position to set this up."

"Do you think he can be trusted?"

Jones nodded. "Yes. Otherwise, there would be a full-blown war in Ukraine right now."

"What if he sets this up and then turns the tables on you?" Hunt asked.

"It's a chance I have to take. I can't run forever." He looked at the men watching him. "Well, say something, damn it."

Hunt nodded. "I'm in, sir."

"Me too," said Striker.

"You can count on me, sir," Rucker agreed.

Jones shifted his gaze to Anvil. "Son?"

"Just point me in the right direction, General, and turn me loose."

"All right then." He picked up the phone.

"General?"

"Two missions for you, Boomer."

"Just name it, Hank."

"Get that canary of yours back to the States," Jones told him.

"Consider it done. What's the second?"

"That might be a little harder."

———————

2nd Battalion, 503rd Infantry Regiment, HQ, Ukraine

"Sorry for the late call, Rad, but being late might work to our benefit."

"Never too late, Boomer. What can I do for you?"

"I need you to put your canary on a plane to the States," Joseph told him.

"To where?"

"I'll reach out to my guys once they're airborne. Send them with him."

"Sure, Boomer, I'll let you know when they're wheels up."

"Thanks, Rad."

———————

Washington, DC

President Nelson looked up from his work and watched Alex Joseph enter the room. The door closed behind him, and he approached the desk. Nelson studied the man for a moment before Joseph said, "Thanks for seeing me on such short notice, Mister President."

"That's not a problem, Alex. I always try to make time for my top people. Besides, you've got me intrigued."

"Sir?"

"Well, for you to ask to see me like this, I figure there must be something rather important you want to discuss."

"There is, sir. A matter of national security."

Nelson frowned. He reached for his phone. "Do I need—"

"No, sir. Please. I need you to hear me out on your own."

"All right then, Alex. Speak."

"Sir, I'm here on behalf of General Hank Jones. He—"

"You what?" Nelson growled as darkness clouded his face.

"Sir, just hear me out."

"The hell I will. If you know where he is, you're duty-bound to tell me."

"Yes, sir."

"Yes, sir, what?"

"Yes, sir, I'll tell you where he is, just as soon as you hear me out."

"What is this, Alex?" Nelson snapped.

"I'm trying to tell you, Mister President."

"Then speak, damn it."

"Sir, we have evidence that the whole Ukraine saga has been a setup all along," Joseph explained.

"It what?"

"I'm telling you the truth, sir. We have the pictures to prove it."

Joseph reached into his pocket and took out a thumb drive. "Take a look at these, sir."

Nelson snatched the thing from him and opened the laptop on his desk. He inserted the drive and clicked on something Joseph couldn't see. Nelson looked up and snapped, "What am I looking at?"

Joseph walked around the desk so he could peer over Nelson's shoulder. "All I see are pictures of nothing."

"That's just it, sir. There was nothing ever there. These pictures are from a satellite that passed over the place the Russian incursion was reported to be. As you can see, there is nothing there."

"I saw them."

"Like you said, sir, pictures can be doctored."

"But who would do that?"

"I can't say, sir," Joseph said. "But we also have evidence that the plane that was shot down was not taken out by the Russians."

"Show me."

"I can't do that, sir. However, if you agree to meet with General Jones, he will be able to show it to you."

"What? And have him kill me too?"

"The general thought you'd think like that. It's why he said for you to bring your secret service detail. Once you arrive, he will turn himself into your custody."

"This smells of an ambush to me," Nelson growled.

"Sir, those pictures came from the DIA. I reached out personally to a friend of mine there who found this for me."

"How do I know that they are what you say they are, Alex?" Nelson asked.

"People have already tried to take them, sir. Been killed for them, in fact."

"Where?"

Joseph said nothing, but he could see the President's mind ticking over. Then, "Wyoming? Is that where?"

Joseph nodded. "Yes, sir."

The expression on Nelson's face changed. "When and where?"

"Three days, sir. I'll let you know. But sir, you can only bring your detail, no one else. It is imperative you understand that."

"Will you be there?"

"If you want me to be, sir."

Nelson nodded. "All right, Alex, you've got your meeting."

"Thank you, sir."

"And when it's over, you resign. I want only people I can trust working for me."

"Yes, sir."

Nelson watched him leave and then stared at the pictures still on his screen. He frowned and then picked up his phone. He said, "Get the director of the Defense Intelligence Agency over here now."

"You need to find out where that meeting is," Clarissa said after listening to the recording.

"I can make it look like he had a heart attack while he was screwing his intern," Brewer told her.

"No. We find out where the meeting is. We kill Jones and the others. Get the evidence, and that's it."

"What about Nelson?"

"We make it look like Jones set up an ambush for him."

"But how do we explain it away?"

"We'll work something out. Put a team together and have them ready to go when needed."

"I'd still like to know what this other evidence is," Brewer said.

"You and me both."

Chase Monaghan sat opposite the president and stared at the computer screen Nelson had turned for him to see. "I need these verified by you," the President told him.

"I can do that for you right now, sir," Monaghan replied.

"Well? Are they real?"

The DIA director nodded. "I saw the exact same

ones the day you ordered troops to Ukraine."

Nelson's hard stare focused on the man's face. He said, "Why wasn't I told about this?"

"If you remember, sir, you made an executive decision without consulting anyone else."

This was his fault. "So, the moves I made were the first in this fucking war. Is that right?"

"We're not at war yet, sir. More like thrust and maneuver."

"Jesus Christ, what have I done?"

"It's not too late to turn it off, sir."

The door opened, and the new Chairman of the Joint Chiefs walked into the room. Nelson didn't worry about hiding his annoyance at being interrupted. "What do you want?"

"Sir, there's been a development in Romania."

"What kind of development?"

"May I turn your television on, sir?"

"I suppose so."

The large screen came on, and pictures of large fires raging in the darkness of night appeared. A ticker rolled along the bottom, saying something about twenty dead and oil fields. "Is this Romania?" Nelson asked.

"Yes, sir. It is one of their oil fields. It was attacked and destroyed a few hours ago."

Nelson looked over at Monaghan. "Verify this."

Monaghan picked up the handset from the president's desk and called his office.

Winkler looked more than a little put out. "Sir, I can assure you that this is true. What we need to be doing is putting people in Romania to help guard the oil wells."

"I already took your advice once—"

"It's legit, Mister President," the DIA director interrupted.

"Who was it?"

"My office is saying they were Russian."

"Like I said, Mister President," Winkler pressed. "We need to get people into Romania to help out."

"More troops, Mister Chairman?"

Winkler shook his head. "No, sir. I'd suggest we could use private contractors who would act as security."

Nelson raised his eyebrows. "Private contractors?"

"Yes, sir. That would free up our own troops and not put the Romanian government under pressure to explain why a foreign power has troops on their soil."

Nelson nodded. "All right, look into it. I'll reach out to the prime minister and see if we can reach an agreement for us to help. Chase, see what your office can dig up."

"Yes, sir."

"He went for it," Winkler told Clarissa. "The contractors are being deployed as we speak."

"Good. I will let the others know."

"There is something else. Nelson is having the DIA look into the attack."

"Should I be worried about anything?" Clarissa asked, her forehead lined as she raised an eyebrow.

"I don't think so."

"Good. How long before the private contractors arrive on the ground?"

"Some should be there within the next twenty-four hours. The rest, within forty-eight."

Clarissa nodded, happy with the news. Things were progressing satisfactorily. With the contractors on the ground, the next part of the plan could be put into operation. She was about to speak again when a ping rang out from the laptop computer in front of her. Looking down at the screen, she saw that there was mail in her secondary email account. Opening the email, she saw just one word. "Panggilan."

Clarissa looked at Winkler. "I have to go."

———————

"What is it?" Clarissa asked, annoyed at the interruption.

The bank of screens before her had each of the Cabal leaders waiting on her for their emergency meeting. "There has been a change of plans." It was

Athena who spoke.

Fucking bitch. "Why wasn't I informed?"

"You are being informed now."

"What part of the plan has been changed?"

"We received a message from a Romanian friend. Actually, it was more like an offer."

"An offer for what?" Clarissa asked, her voice unable to hide her disdain.

There was a smug look upon Athena's face. "One that will benefit us greatly."

"Oh, for fuck sake, just tell me already. Who the fuck do you think you are?"

Athena's dark eyes flared. "Careful, dear. Remember who we are."

"Remember who *I* fucking am and why I was put here. I have great reach, and you, *dear*, are not beyond it."

"Enough of the bickering," Adonis said in a loud voice. "Within the next week, there will be a coup within the Romanian government. It shall be fully backed and aided by us. In return, we gain all of the drilling rights to the new oil field."

Clarissa was shocked. She'd spent a long time devising the elements of her plan, and it all came down to a simple coup. "So, the war with Russia will be unnecessary? Is that what you are saying?"

"No, the war will go ahead. We need a regime change in Russia so we can unite Europe. With that done, we can work on ridding ourselves of the European Union and have our own model put into place. Only then will we control all of Europe, after which we can focus our attention on China and North Korea."

"I will have to concentrate on furthering the action against Russia," Clarissa told the other members, most of whom remained taciturn at her proclamation. "If I had not wasted so much of my time putting the Romanian part into effect, we would have had troops crossing the frontier."

Her voice held an edge of bitterness, and it didn't go unnoticed. "We apologize for that, but it has only just transpired, and there was no time to consult you," Hades tried to explain.

"What is it you propose to do?" Adonis asked.

"Give me a couple of days and you'll see," Clarissa said curtly.

She disconnected abruptly, pissed at the way they had all gone behind her back. She sat in silence, contemplating having Brewer send one of his men to make an example of Athena, who she was certain was instrumental in the deviation from their set program. But should she venture on that course of action, the others might, out of concern for themselves, retaliate and send people after her. No, she had to let things run for a while, keeping a keen eye on progress. Not one to let nature take its course, if there was no improvement in short order, she would reassert her authority and handle things herself.

Taking out her encrypted cell, she called Brewer. "We're going to need your best Russian-speaking operatives."

"What are we going to do with them?"

"Kill the President and start a war."

"I'll see what I can do."

CHAPTER 17

Falkenburg, Austria

The team had been back in Austria for ten hours and had used most of that time to rest. Thurston had been thoroughly checked over by Morales, who had initially fussed over her health and wellbeing, and was now sleeping.

Ferrero called Arenas and Kane aside to discuss plans with them. Once he had them on their own, he said, "I don't know about you, but I'm sick and tired of being on the receiving end. I've had Slick run down some of the names of the international Cabal people, and I think we've narrowed down the top echelon of the whole thing."

Kane sensed where this was going and suggested, "You want us to take them out?"

"Yes. I'm not going to order you to do it, but it would go a long way toward bringing the whole rotting structure crashing down."

"Do we know who Ares is yet?"

"No. I'm hoping to obtain that information as we go along. I have been in contact with Hank Jones, who mentioned that a meeting has been set up between him and President Nelson. They have evidence the President needs to see. It could help the general's cause."

"Let's hope so. Does he know about your plan?" Kane asked.

Ferrero nodded.

Kane looked at Arenas. "What do you think, Carlos?"

"How about we get the team together, *amigo*, and see what we can come up with?"

"Include Traynor," Kane said. "That'll even out the numbers if we go ahead with it."

"You might want to include MI6 too," Ferrero suggested.

"All right, let's do it."

"I'll get you what you need."

Bancroft placed six pictures on the table before them. Each face had a name hand-written above it. He stabbed a straightened finger at the first one, a man in his mid-forties with dark hair. "Wolfgang Schmidt. German. Federal Minister of Defense. Ex armed forces. Has a bodyguard of two and is as regular as clockwork when it comes to doing things."

Kane looked at Axe. "You and Traynor want this guy?"

"Sure, why not?"

"Bancroft will supply you with everything you need to get the job done."

The MI6 man pointed to the second picture, this one of a woman with long black hair and a pretty face. "Licia Barone. Italian Ministry of Justice. She has a tendency to go out at night, visiting clubs that accommodate the same sex. Or she dials in. That is about her only weakness."

Kane looked at Cara. "I'm sorry, but—"

She nodded. "I can do it. Wouldn't be the first time I've kissed a girl."

Knocker opened his mouth to speak.

"Or shot someone," she said, cutting off whatever words he was going to speak.

Instead, he pointed at the next one. "I want her."

"Who is she?" Kane asked.

"Ellen frigging Grayson. She used to be an officer in the old Essex Regiment. A colonel if I remember rightly. She was a hard cow. Good officer, though, right up until she wasn't. Rumors began circulating that she had some prisoners shot. Soon after that, she discharged and went to MI6."

Knocker gave Bancroft a sidelong glance. The man nodded and continued the story. "She took over black ops, commanding a section performing jobs no other section wanted to touch. The dirtier, the better. Knocker was being too kind when he called her a cow."

"What does she do?"

"She's head of MI6."

"Shit," Kane muttered.

"Don't worry, you're all safe here. If you weren't, she'd be crawling up our asses by now."

"You and Brick, Knocker?'

Knocker shook his head. "No, just me. No offense, Brick old mate, but this requires the finesse of a one-man job."

"None taken," Brick replied.

"All right," said Kane. "That still leaves Brick out in the cold."

"Belgium or France?" Bancroft asked.

"What's the third option?" Brick countered.

"Australia."

"Now, that—"

"Forget it," Kane said.

"Have you ever been to Belgium?" Bancroft asked.

"No."

"Good. You and I will be going there."

"Then that's settled. It's a good place to start."

"When do we leave?" Axe asked.

"Right now," Kane replied. "Pack light."

Berlin, Germany

Pete Traynor and Axe sat in a black Audi RS Q8 across the street from a small pizza restaurant called Pizza *auf der älteren Straße*. Intel had Schmidt coming to the place on the same day each week. As luck had it, it was that day, and being a creature of habit, he rarely missed his standing reservation.

When he arrived, it was in a late model Mercedes Benz. One bodyguard was driving, the other riding shotgun. It was assumed that both would be armed. What they didn't know was whether the pair were Cabal like their boss or just hired muscle for State protection. Traynor took a picture as they climbed out of the Mercedes and sent it through the ether to Swift for identification. They sat and waited for several minutes until the reply came back. "Considered to be hostile. Treat as such."

"What's the plan?" Axe asked him.

"If we wait until they come out, it should be easier. Plus, it's less likely that innocents will get caught in the crossfire."

"OK, we wait."

They didn't have to wait long. A large explosion rocked the pizza place, and the windows blew out in a flash of orange flame. Glass and debris erupted across the street, cutting down pedestrians as they walked past. Bodies were flung around, one coming through the window with the blast. The concussion rocked the Audi, and both men ducked as debris began peppering their vehicle.

After the initial blast, they looked up to see the roof of the restaurant cave in.

All along the street, car alarms had been activated, blaring out their various rotations of noise; screams and cries of pain from the injured started to echo. Axe saw a person stagger out of the rubble of the pizza restaurant, missing an arm. He looked at Traynor and said, "What the fuck just happened, man?"

"Someone beat us to the punch, Axe. Come on."

"Where we going?"

"We have to help these people," Traynor said, opening the door of the Audi.

"Yeah, we do."

Falkenburg, Austria

"What happened?" Ferrero asked.

"Someone beat us to it," Traynor told him. "They had obviously researched his movements just as we did. They planted a bomb and detonated it."

"I'll have Swift wash through whatever footage he can find and see what he can come up with. Was there anything else?"

"I'm just wondering if this could be the start of something," Traynor said.

"You mean, someone who has the same idea as us?"

"Something like that."

"Who knows? I'll tell the others to be on the lookout."

Brussels, Belgium

Minister of the Interior Christian Dirkson left his office and unlocked his BMW with its fob from ten meters out. He opened the door, leaned across to place his briefcase on the passenger seat, and made himself comfortable in the plush leather bucket seat behind the wheel before pressing the ignition button. As an independent government official, he relied on no one to see to his needs, and it had been that way since his election—less drain on the public purse. The cost-cutting measures meant a decrease in his security, providing easy access for those responsible for placing a bomb under his vehicle. The explosion was loud and violent. It blew out windows in the immediate vicinity and killed a couple of pedestrians.

Waiting down the street half a block in an Alfa Romeo, Brick and Bancroft felt the concussive blast as it washed over the vehicle. The orange explosion was replaced by a pall of black smoke. Civilians died, cut to pieces by the hot, razor-sharp debris sent in every direction by the bomb.

After the initial noise subsided, the cries of the injured and maimed took its place. Two people had been removed from the list.

London, England

Knocker waited and watched for Ellen Grayson to emerge from the SIS building in Vauxhall. He'd been there for two hours, sitting in the darkened Volvo XC90 and waiting for his target to appear. Beside him on the passenger seat was a suppressed P226. It had been rendered untraceable and would be discarded on completion of the job.

Those two hours had given him time to reflect upon the only time he and Ellen had crossed paths. He'd been conducting a mission in Yugoslavia, the target a Yugoslav arms dealer suspected of having a biological agent in his possession that had been advertised on the dark web. Knocker had been able to trace the seller and had located him, along with his wife and children.

When Knocker reported his findings, the kill order came down. Upon querying it, he was told there was no mistake. His mission now included the whole family. Knocker's reply was a polite fuck you.

Grayson, having perceived that he would take issue with his new orders, had a backup plan in place. Within the hour, a Hellfire missile blew the shit out of the residence, killing all within.

Knocker being Knocker, he went on a rampage back at the SIS building, getting past four men before he was stopped from doing the same to the MI6 commander. For the rest of his MI6 career, all of his orders were relayed through a different handler.

He was brought back to the present when the black Range Rover appeared. It flashed under the streetlights and turned onto Vauxhall Bridge road.

Knocker eased into the traffic and began tailing Grayson's chauffeured ride across the Thames. The SUV turned onto Drummond Gate, which in turn changed to Bessborough Street. Knocker followed them as that changed into Lupus Street. The Range Rover slowed and signaled before turning right onto Winchester.

Knocker took the turn behind them and then sped up, the engine grumbled in protest and the rear end sitting down as it picked up speed. He was just about to overtake when a motorbike appeared on his right.

Knocker frowned and eased off the gas, watching as the bike shot up beside the Range Rover into the blind spot. He saw the rider reach out and place something on the rear quarter panel, then speed up and leave the vehicle in his wake.

The SAS man slammed on the brakes as a thought occurred to him, and the Volvo shuddered to a halt in the middle of the street.

Up ahead, the Range Rover was engulfed in a devastating explosion, blown apart by a tremendous force that was catastrophic for all within.

"Fuck me," he breathed. Looking past the burning pyre, he saw that the individual responsible for the ruination sat on their bike, checking out their handiwork.

Knocker's face hardened, and he stomped on the gas pedal hard enough for the force to jar up his leg. Tires squealed as the SUV powered forward. Sure, it had been his mission to terminate Grayson, but he wanted to know who this new player was and why they'd done what they did.

He navigated around the burning wreck, his focus on the bike rider, whose attention he had drawn with his speedy advance in their direction.

The rider turned and opened the throttle wide on the bike. The powerful machine spun its back wheel before rocketing forward, its front wheel coming clear of the asphalt.

Knocker gave the Volvo as much gas as it would take, trying to run the rider down. Up ahead, the bike turned left onto Sussex Street. The SAS man trod on the brake pedal hard and turned the wheel, and the rear of the SUV slid around until its nose was pointed toward the fleeing bike and rider. As soon as the Volvo had straightened, the gas pedal went down again, and Knocker continued the chase.

As the vehicle hammered along Sussex Street, the street lamps flashed off the windscreen, briefly illuminating and dimming the interior of the SUV like a strobe. The bike's brake lights came on, and it turned right onto Sutherland Street.

Knocker followed the bike around and watched as the rider opened the throttle to full and left him in its wake.

At the intersection of Sutherland Street and Warwick Way was a painted roundabout. Both the pursuer and pursued were traveling in excess of one hundred when they reached it. The bike laid over just enough to negotiate the turn. However, Knocker realized with alarm almost too late that there was no way the Volvo was going to negotiate the turn without pain.

He virtually stood on the brakes, pulling back on the wheel like an equestrian would his reins to try to stop his mount. At the last moment, Knocker yanked hard on the wheel, and the Volvo flipped. Every airbag deployed to cushion the blows of the violently rolling SUV, but somehow it wasn't enough.

Pain ripped through the SAS man as the vehicle came to a stop, the battered Volvo upside-down on the street.

Knocker groaned, trying to regain his senses, which seemed to have been thrust in every direction. He could smell gas and taste coppery blood in his mouth. After a few moments, he realized the vehicle was inverted and that he was hanging by the seatbelt.

"Cock!" He groaned aloud. "Useless fucking cock."

Operating on muscle memory, he reached around and released the seatbelt, and immediately regretted not having thought it through. As he landed on his head, the pain in his body increased, and he growled, "Jesus Christ."

His knees smacked him hard in the chest, and he was forced to wriggle around in the broken glass of the roof's interior so he could crawl out through what had been the driver's side window.

With more than a little pained effort, he managed to extricate himself from the wreck. He climbed to his feet and leaned against the Volvo as he got his bearings. He heard a voice call to him, "Hey, mate, are you all right?"

Knocker looked along the street where the bike had disappeared. "Never fucking better," he mumbled.

Now all he had to do was find the suppressed handgun and get out of there before the police turned up.

Rome, Italy

"Reaper, where's Cara?" Ferrero's voice sounded urgent.

"She's inside the club, why?"

"Get her out of there now."

"Why, what's happening?" Kane asked.

"They're all being assassinated," Ferrero said hurriedly. "Over the past two nights, every target on our list except for Licia has died. Even the couple we haven't marked are done."

"Who is doing it?"

"We have no idea. We assume Ares, but until we confirm who that is, we're shit out of ideas."

"I'll—" He stopped and watched as two SUVs pulled up outside the club entrance and six men emerged wearing long coats and carrying automatic weapons. They shot the two men on the door and went inside.

"I have to go, Luis. Looks like the warning came a bit late."

Kane grabbed his and Cara's handguns and emerged quickly from the vehicle they'd rented, then ran across the street toward the club. By the time he stepped onto the sidewalk, the shooting inside had already begun.

—————

Cara felt Licia's hand move up her thigh, pushing the hem of her already short skirt higher. It hadn't taken long for her to reel in her bait. A tight red dress that covered just enough featuring a deep v-neckline exposing an appropriate amount of breast without being slutty was her attire, and being in the right place at the right time had ensured she was noticed.

The bonus was that Cara spoke Italian with an attractive clumsiness that appealed to the woman who now nuzzled her exposed neck.

Licia happened to be a couple of years older than Cara, which placed her in the right age bracket to be fair game for the wanton government minister.

The hand moving up Cara's thigh continued to climb the exterior of the dress to her right breast. The Italian woman squeezed it gently and felt the nipple harden under her touch. She suddenly pinched it and mistook Cara's gasp as one of pleasure instead of pain.

Licia eased back and smiled, a lustful look on her face, and had leaned in to kiss Cara when the gunfire erupted.

Reacting instinctively, Cara dragged the shocked Licia to the floor. The woman's two bodyguards shot out of their booth next to the one the women were in, only to be mown down by a storm of bullets. Licia tried to move beneath Cara, who spoke forcefully into her ear. "Stay the fuck down if you want to live." She wondered why she'd chosen those words since she and Kane were here to kill her.

All around them, women were being taken down. Screams of fear and pain echoed through the large room as the music died. A body thudded close to where Cara lay with Licia. The dead woman was blonde, her blue eyes open in death, blood spattered on her once-pretty face, now marred by a bullet hole.

Licia screamed and virtually threw Cara clear of her. Then, without regard for safety, she rose to her feet to run.

Cara heard a shout. It was English, and she could make out the accent. As she watched, the shooters trained their guns at Licia. Their intent was unmistakable; they were here to kill the Italian woman.

Within moments, a handgun joined the fray. Cara's head snapped around, and she saw Kane standing with his feet apart near the entrance.

Two shooters dropped where they stood. Kane shifted his aim and fired again, a bullet snapping back the head of a third shooter.

Cara knew that once the remaining three shooters concentrated their fire on Kane, he was as good as dead. She came to her feet and moved briskly to one of Licia's fallen bodyguards. She dug under the dead man's coat and found his personal weapon, a Glock. She racked the slide to make sure that there was a round in the chamber and opened fire.

A fourth shooter fell from accurate fire, the weapon in his hands hitting the floor just before he did. The death of their accomplice split the last two shooters. They were both armed with MP5s and were unloading their magazines at an alarming rate.

Cara dived for the floor as round after round impacted around her. By sheer dumb luck, not one bullet hit her. Then the incoming rounds stopped. She glanced up quickly and saw the shooter reloading. Cara raised the Glock and fired three times, each impact drawing a reaction from the shooter, who eventually fell to the floor. The shooting stopped, but not the screaming. Cara looked for Kane and saw him standing like a beacon amid turbulent seas. She climbed to her feet, and her gaze took in the carnage in the room. She saw Licia's body on the floor.

Cara hurried over and touched her. The woman screamed in fear as she turned her head and recognized Cara. Realization hit her, and she said, "Go! We must go!"

Cara helped her to her feet and ushered her toward Kane and the door. He saw them coming and said to Cara, "What are you doing?"

"I have an idea."

They moved Licia through the doorway and out onto the sidewalk. They were about to cross the road when the sharp crack of a rifle split the night. The Italian women grunted and stumbled.

"She's hit," Cara cried, taking her weight.

Licia's knees buckled, and Cara dragged her behind the vehicle the shooters had arrived in as a second round came in and ricocheted off the asphalt.

Kane joined them and looked at the buildings opposite the club to find the shooter. Beside him, Cara crouched over Licia, trying to stop the flow of blood. Kane glared at her. "What the fuck are you doing?" he demanded.

"I'm trying to save her fucking life."

"Why?"

She ignored him. Licia had been shot through the left lung, which was rapidly filling with blood. What other internal damage had been done was anyone's guess, but something vital other than the lung had been hit because the woman was shaking and her face was changing color.

"Licia, can you hear me?" Cara asked as another bullet from the sniper hammered into the vehicle they had sheltered behind. "Licia, can you hear me?"

The woman nodded.

"Tell me, who is Ares?"

Her eyes hardened and she stared at Cara suspiciously.

Kane called to her, "Tell her that all the others are dead. Someone killed them."

Cara stared at Kane. "What? Aren't—"

"No, it wasn't us. Just tell her," he said firmly.

"Did you hear that, Licia? They're all dead.

Someone killed them. They sent these men here to kill you."

The dying woman stared at Cara in silence.

"Do you understand me? Someone killed everyone. You're the last. Tell me who Ares is."

Her lips parted. "Th—that bitch."

"Who?"

"A-ares."

"Yes, who is Ares?"

"Cla-Clarissa Rhodes," she replied.

Cara nodded. "Thank you."

"Kill-kill the bitch," Licia said, then began coughing as a torrent of blood flowed from her mouth. Her body went limp, and she closed her eyes.

"Reaper, I have a name," Cara called to Kane as he fired a couple of shots in the shooter's general direction.

"What?" he called back.

"Ares. I have Ares' name."

Another round slammed into the vehicle in protest of Cara's words, then came the sirens from the approaching emergency responders. As they grew closer, the shooting stopped. Kane looked down at Licia's body and said to Cara, "It's time we were not here."

CHAPTER 18

Falkenburg, Austria

"This is Clarissa Rhodes," Ferrero told the team. "She's the Speaker of the House back home, and given the intel we were able to get from Licia Barone before she died, the one and only Ares."

Each member of the team had made it back from their missions in good time, if a little confused.

"I thought—" Axe started.

"The new one, Axe," Ferrero said. "That we must assume."

"And she's in the frame for killing all the others?" Brick asked.

A door opened, and Knocker walked gingerly into the room they were using for the briefing. Outwardly, only a few cuts and abrasions from the crash were evident. However, beneath the surface, he hurt like a bitch. Morales looked at him and scowled. "I thought I told you to rest?"

"I'll get some later, Doc. Right now, I've got a briefing to attend."

Reynolds rose from the chair she was seated on, offering it to her beat-up teammate. "Take this, sweetie. You look like you could use it."

"I feel like I've been run over by a Waterloo double-decker," he replied as he sat down. "Thanks."

"Right," said Ferrero. "Getting back to your question, Brick. Yes, she's the only one still alive out of what we assume were all the top-ranking officials in the Cabal."

"Why would the silly cow take them all out?" Knocker asked.

"Total control," Bancroft said. "As it was, they all controlled their piece of the Cabal. This leaves the door open for one person to take over. Nothing like total control."

"Does General Jones know?" Teller asked.

"Yes," Kane answered. "He has a secret meeting with the President in the next fifteen hours to try and convince him this was all one big global conspiracy that we had nothing to do with."

"What do we do?" Axe asked.

"We go home." All eyes turned toward Thurston, who was walking into the room much the same way Knocker had. The SAS man made to rise to give up his seat, but he was stopped by Traynor. "Sit here, General."

She smiled and nodded. "Thanks, Pete."

Thurston winced as she lowered herself to the hard plastic chair. She ran her gaze over those she could see and said, "Luis and I have talked it over, and we're headed back to the States in a couple of hours."

"They'll be waiting for us, ma'am," Cara pointed out.

"Oh, we won't be blowing a bugle or sending out a marching band, be sure of that. Reaper Team will be dropping into Wyoming to link up with General Jones. The rest of us will be touching down in a place called Willow Forks."

"Oh, God, no," Teller groaned.

"Is there a problem, Master Sergeant?" Thurston asked him.

"Apart from the fact that it's in the middle of bum fu…in the middle of nowhere, ma'am, no problem."

"That's why we chose it. I take it you know what it is?"

"Yes, ma'am."

"How about you enlighten the rest, then."

"Yes, ma'am. Willow Forks is an old airbase in Idaho. It's miles from nowhere and has a runway long enough, or it was long enough, for heavy bombers during the Cold War. By now, the runway should be in a sufficient state of disrepair to lose a C-17 down the potholes in it. Apart from the trees and the bears, it's an absolute paradise. Did I miss anything, ma'am?"

"No, I think you about covered it."

"Why are we dropping in on the general?" Kane asked.

"Carlos," Thurston said.

"You will link up with him to strengthen his position in case the Cabal gets wind of the meeting. He currently has Scimitar and a handful of SEALs with him. Another small team of SEALs will reach him in the next hour, escorting a package, but that won't be enough, hence you and the others, my friend."

Kane nodded. "We'll be cutting it fine."

"That's why we're leaving now," Thurston said. "Get whatever you need to take and move out. Mister Bancroft, thanks for all your help and hospitality."

"My pleasure, General. I trust the ride will suffice."

"I'm sure it will."

———

Washington, DC

Clarissa finished with the report and looked up at Brewer. "Is this for real?"

The director of the CIA nodded. "Every last detail as far as I can tell."

"They're all dead?"

"Yes."

"Is this your doing?" she asked, staring hard

at him.

He held his hands up at shoulder height. "It wasn't us."

"Then it must have been Thurston and her fucking team."

"If it was, they might have done us a favor. *You* a favor."

Clarissa frowned. "How...oh, I see what you mean."

"It leaves you and you alone at the head of the most powerful organization the globe has ever seen."

"First we have to get through the next few days," Clarissa pointed out. "Have you organized a team?"

"Yes. They will be ready and waiting when I join them."

"Fine. We need this to go smoothly, or it will spell the end for us."

"It will," Brewer assured her.

"Let's hope so."

When Brewer got up to leave, Clarissa watched his retreating form until the door closed behind him. Now that she was on her own, she reached for the encrypted cell in her top drawer and dialed a number she'd memorized. As she waited for it to be answered, she leaned back in her swivel chair and crossed her shapely legs.

"Yes."

"Are you ready?"

"Yes."

"If this goes bad, I want you to kill him immediately. Then make sure it all leads back to him. They must think he is Ares."

"Understood."

Outside Jackson, Wyoming

"Senior Chief Nick Dawson, sir. My men call me Skywalker."

Hank Jones shook his hand. "Glad to have you aboard, Senior Chief."

Dawson stepped aside. "This is Tyler, Tank Brown, and Daisy Philips, sir."

"You still humping that handle around with you, Daisy?" Striker asked the SEAL.

"Can't seem to shake it."

"Suits if you ask me," Ruggles growled.

Turning to face the man, he said, "Damn, Master Chief, ain't you dead yet?"

"Not damn well likely, son. Only the good die young, so you're looking at an immortal man."

"More like an amoral one," Hunt growled.

"I'm sure I didn't hear that, Butter Knife. Good to see you again, Skywalker."

"I take it you know Master Chief Ruggles," Jones surmised.

"Master Chief has been around forever, sir. They

say the dinosaurs were killed by a meteor. Word is it was a SEAL with a big knife."

"You saying I'm old, Skywalker?"

"No, sir. I'm saying you're a frigging dinosaur."

Ruggles laughed. "And still able to kick all your asses, singularly or together."

Dawson looked at the general. "I'd believe him, sir. If he says he can do it, it's usually true."

"I believe you, Dawson. I believe you. Now for the serious stuff."

Eyes all turned to the man in chains, who'd parachuted in with the team on a double harness strapped to Tank Brown. "I take it this is our man."

"That's him, sir."

"What's your name?" Jones asked.

The man mumbled something incoherent, and one of Tank's meaty hands slapped him on the back of his head. "Cole Myers, General," he said in a clear voice.

Tyler said, "He's still suffering from the effects of the B-52 strike. Lucky he's still alive."

"At least he can talk."

Tyler looked around and asked, "Is this everyone?"

"For the moment," Jones replied. "Kane and his team will be here soon, I hope."

"I've never met this Kane. Have certainly heard a lot about him, though."

"He and his team are good people to go downrange with," Hunt told him. "You remember Brick Peters?"

Tyler nodded. "Yeah, I think I do."

"He's the team's combat medic."

Tyler nodded.

"All right, let's get this guy put away somewhere secure. Chief Hunt, you need to get out to the drop zone," Jones said. Then to Tyler, "You men want some chow?"

"You got any, sir?'

"We might be able to scrape the hide off something for you."

"That'd be great."

Over Wyoming

The C-17 rear ramp lowered slowly in anticipation of the five people about to jump from twenty thousand feet. All had on equipment supplied by Bancroft before they left Austria. The plane had been rerouted from Ramstein to Austria to pick up the team before continuing the journey to the US. It would drop Kane and his team in Wyoming before doubling back to Idaho.

That had been the plan until a certain master sergeant pointed out that it would be more beneficial for the plane to be utilized as an aerial platform to operate from, providing they had enough of a fuel load to do so.

Thurston and Ferrero had agreed to the suggestion, and once they reached out to Joseph, it was all sorted—even a mid-air refuel that would add to their flight time. The pallet of supplies was pushed out into the daylight and disappeared beyond the ramp. It was quickly followed by the team, Kane giving Arenas a thumbs up as he led them out.

Once more unto the breach.

Outside of Jackson, Wyoming

"We come bearing gifts," Kane said to Hunt as he shook his hand. "How is it, Scimitar?"

"Fucked up beyond all recognition, Reaper. Absolutely FUBAR."

"How's your team?"

Hunt nodded somberly. "We lost Popeye."

"Shit."

"We picked up a few Team guys along the way, along with a fucking dinosaur."

Kane gave him a puzzled look and cocked an eyebrow. Hunt said, "You'll see. We need to get this stuff into the truck. There's work to do."

"Let's do it."

Hunt saw Cara looking over the crate, checking that it was intact. "How are you doing, darlin'?"

She looked at him and smiled. "Baby, I'm ready

for whatever comes next."

She walked over and gave him a hug. "Good to see you, Bord."

"You too."

"Unhand her, asshole," Brick called. "She's ours. Get your own weapons specialist."

"Hey, I got a surprise for you when we get back."

"Really? What is it?"

Hunt looked knowingly at Kane. "You'll see."

"Well, look what the cat drug in," Ruggles said with a mirthless grin.

"Shit, ain't you dead yet?" Brick asked the master chief. "I can help you on your way if you like. Give you an OD of morphine."

"Son, I live on that shit."

"I gather you two know each other," Cara observed.

"Biggest prick to ever put on an instructor's t-shirt. Eats nails and shits barbed wire, ma'am."

"You take no notice of him, ma'am, I'm just a big teddy bear until these assholes get on my good side."

Hunt looked at Cara. "If I was you, I'd leave now before they start making goo-goo eyes at each other."

Kane was talking to Striker, Jones, and Dawson about how they planned to play the next mission. Kane said, "I know they won't be expecting my team,

General. How about you use us as a quick reaction force? We'll hole up just in case shit goes down."

Jones nodded. "Sounds good to me."

"You got a sniper, Reaper?" Dawson asked.

"Yeah, I got me a good one."

Knocker approached the small group. "Hey, General, how's your dog's dinner going down?"

Jones' eyes narrowed. "I see you haven't fragged his British ass yet."

Kane smiled. "If I had, we wouldn't be here today. His contact at MI6 helped us no end."

Striker stared at the SAS man and asked, "What the fuck is—"

"Don't do it?" Kane warned him.

"—a 'dog's dinner?'"

Knocker's eyes sparkled as a grin split his face. "You aren't related to Axe, are you?"

"Shit," Kane breathed.

"What?" Striker asked.

Knocker turned to see Axe standing not far away. "Hey, Axe, I found your brother."

"Fuck you, you dodgy shitting scouser."

"Knocker," Kane said firmly. "Go and find something to do before you convert everyone to your British ways."

"And that's a bad thing? Learning the Queen's English—"

"Cara!"

She looked at the group and knew what was

happening. "Don't make me come over there, Ray."

"Shit, she called me 'Ray.'"

The SAS man wandered off, his fun done. Striker asked Kane, "What the hell was that?"

"That's just Knocker being Knocker. Point him in the right direction and turn him loose, and he's a top-tier operator."

"I like him," Dawson said. "Is he like that under fire?"

"Sometimes I think he's worse."

"Now I *really* like him."

"That's great," Jones growled. "We've worked out who likes or dislikes the SAS man. Now, can we get back to the mission? We've only got an hour until the President shows."

"Have you got somewhere picked out?"

"Yes, there's a good LZ that they're utilizing about two klicks from here."

"Let's go, then," Kane said. "The sooner, the better."

Jones' face hardened. "Just so we all understand, I'm not coming back from this. Whether he believes us or not, I'm turning myself in. Understood?"

They all nodded their agreement and broke up. Kane walked over to speak to Cara and Knocker. "How was it?" she asked.

"You'll need to work your magic for us if this goes bad. Whatever happens, the President stays alive." He looked at Knocker. "That's your job. I want you to go with the others. You'll be Nelson's new best friend."

"Are you expecting trouble?" Cara asked.

"I have a feeling that won't go away. An opportunity like this will be too much for the Cabal to pass up, and as we know, they have a knack of finding shit out."

"Don't worry, Reaper, I'll be so far up his ass he'll think my name is 'Enema.'"

CHAPTER 19

Outside Jackson, Wyoming

The helicopter's engine wound down and the rotor slowed to a stop. Nelson had forgone the use of Air Force One for a DIA-supplied Gulfstream G280 and then a Bell 525 helicopter. More chance of keeping things below the radar that way, he figured.

The first to disembark from the helicopter were the six men of Nelson's protection detail, followed by the President and then Rear Admiral Alex Joseph. The detail spread out and formed a wide perimeter around the Nelson as he walked toward Jones and the others.

Nelson and his detail stopped and waited for the others to come forward. Jones moved toward him with Knocker, the prisoner, and Hunt on his other side. The rest of the SEALs fanned out in a wider perimeter than the one the Secret Service detail had formed.

On a ridge in the trees to the southeast, Cara sighted through the scope of a .375 CheyTac Intervention Sniper System. Toward the base of the slope were the rest of the team, waiting and watching.

Knocker heard Cara say into her comms, "Reaper Two ready."

Jones and his entourage stopped within six or seven meters of Nelson, and the general looked at Joseph. "Good to see you, Alex."

"You too, Hank."

Knocker approached Nelson, and the Secret Service detail started to pull their weapons.

"Reaper Three, what the fuck are you doing?" Kane whispered harshly into his comms.

"Easy, gentlemen," Knocker said, leaving his 416 in an unthreatening position. He drew level with Nelson and turned to face Jones, who gave him an incredulous look. The SAS man said in his heavy accent, "Mister President, I'm under strict orders to make sure your ass is safe, sir. So, I'm standing post here."

Nelson was stunned by the man's audacity, and his mouth opened and closed a few times before he said, "OK."

"Knocker, you dumb son of a bitch," Axe said softly. "You got some balls."

"Mister President," Jones said, "thank you for meeting with me."

Nelson nodded. "I'm not sure why I did. Meeting with an assassin is—"

"Accused, sir," Knocker said out of the corner of his mouth.

Nelson glared at him. "If you're going to stand there, shut up."

"Yes, sir."

"Mister President, we have proof that I—we—had nothing to do with it."

"Is this it?" Nelson asked, pointing at Myers.

"Yes, sir."

"All right, I'm listening. You've got five minutes to convince me."

"Sir, have you ever heard of the Cabal?"

"Oh, for crying out loud—"

"Excuse me, sir," Jones said. "You gave me five minutes to convince you. You're eating into my time."

Jones went on to give him a condensed version of what had happened from beginning to end. "Sir, you've seen the pictures, so I guess you know about the bombing in Ankara. The person who set Mary Thurston and her people up for it was CIA. Team Reaper was left to burn in Syria, where a mercenary team was to finish them. Mary and her HQ element were handed over to the Turkish authorities, then she was passed on to a triad organization in Hong Kong, where she was beaten and tortured by Chinese State Security. We also know that the plane shot down in Ukraine wasn't taken out by Russian troops but by Americans."

Nelson snorted derisively. "I find that—"

"Sir, five minutes," Knocker said in a low voice.

Nelson glowered at him and Knocker shrugged.

Jones continued, "Myers."

"It's true, sir. We were ordered to shoot or try to shoot down an aircraft."

"By whom?"

"I don't know where the order came from."

"I do," Jones said. "Clarissa Rhodes."

"That's ridiculous," Nelson growled.

"No, sir, it's true. Over the past few days, someone has publicly taken out all the top Cabal people across the globe: Italy, Belgium, Germany, Australia, Great Britain, France, all except the one they called Ares."

"How do you know it was this Cabal you proclaim exists that did it?" Nelson asked.

"Because Mary Thurston's operators were assigned a termination order for some of them."

"You mean, they were going to assassinate them?"

"Just as sure as shit, Mister President. Except someone beat them to it. Every time they moved to terminate, it literally blew up in their faces. Except for one. One of them lived long enough to reveal who Ares was. Do you know what name that was, Mister President?"

Nelson shook his head, but deep down, he knew what was coming. Knew what Jones was saying was true.

"That name was Clarissa Rhodes."

No sooner had the name left Jones' lips when one of the Secret Service agents to Knocker's left started easing his right hand under his coat. The SAS man whispered, "Cara, my left."

Within the space of four heartbeats, three things happened. The agent drew his gun, a .375-caliber bullet punched through his chest, and all hell broke loose.

———————

"Reaper One? Bravo Four, copy?"

"Read you Lima Charlie, Bravo Four."

"We've just picked up signatures on ISR," Swift said clearly. "They're headed your way from the east."

"What kind of signatures, Bravo Four?"

"We think they're incoming tangos."

"How many?"

There was a brief pause before he replied. "I would estimate thirty tangos, Reaper One."

"Shit. Cara, thirty tangos inbound from the east. You pick them up?"

Cara shifted her scope and swept the forest. "I have nothing, Reaper."

"Knocker," Kane whispered into his comms, "we have thirty inbound tangos from the east. Be ready."

For the next few minutes, nothing happened. Kane and the others couldn't even pick up the intruders. Then Knocker's whisper came over the comms to Cara.

"Cara, my left."

She sighted the CheyTac on the Secret Service agent who was moving his hand under his coat. As it reappeared with his handgun, she squeezed the trigger.

———————

As soon as the round hit the would-be assassin, Knocker leaped at Nelson, knocking him to the ground. "Tangos in the trees! Get down!"

As soon as he had Nelson on the ground, automatic weapons fire erupted across the meadow from the tree line. Knocker placed his knee on Nelson's back to hold him down, brought his 416 up, and started searching for targets.

Four of the Secret Service detail fell in the initial burst. With the one that Cara had killed, Nelson was down to only one in his detail.

They weren't the only ones to fall. Myers the prisoner died with two bullets in his chest. Daisy Philips went down with a bullet in the right side of his chest from a round that somehow missed his armor plate. Master Chief Ruggles took a bullet in his left leg but stood like a ramrod, firing at muzzle flashes from the tree line until another one kicked his right leg out from beneath him. From where he knelt,

Knocker wasn't sure which was more disconcerting, the amount of incoming fire or the venom the veteran SEAL was hurling at those who'd shot him.

Next to Jones, Hunt and Rucker were firing at the tree line. Hunt heard Ruggles go down and said above the gunfire, "Go see to him."

As Rucker crawled over to Ruggles to render him aid, Striker and Anvil darted to the right. Hunt knew they were trying to flank whoever was in the tree line.

A cry drew Hunt's attention, and he turned to see Tyler down and squirming on the ground in pain. Dawson was crawling over to him, and bullets were kicking up dirt all around him.

The rate of incoming fire seemed to increase the longer the firefight went on, and they were in danger of being pinned down and wiped out.

Knocker said into his comms, "Reaper, if you're going to do something, now would be a really good frigging time."

———

The CheyTac slammed against Cara's shoulder as she fired another round. The head of a shooter hidden behind a deadfall snapped back before he slumped forward. She shifted her aim and fired at yet another target.

She saw Striker and Anvil break to the right as

they tried to get into a better position, swept her rifle to the left, and saw a shooter in the trees sighting his weapon on the two SEALs as they ran.

Cara squeezed the trigger, and the large caliber bullet punched into the man's side and knocked him off his feet. She noticed the shooter a few meters past him who was also taking aim at the two SEALs. Another round and he too was kneeling before the gates of Hell.

Kane's voice came over the comms. "Cara, we're pushing left to see if we can flank them."

"Roger that."

Then came Knocker's call. To Cara, the unflappable Brit sounded a little off his game. Normally cool and calm no matter the circumstance, his voice held a certain edge.

Cara said, "Reaper Three, this is Reaper Two, copy?"

"You calling to chat me up, Reaper Two?"

He sounded breathless. "Are you OK, Knocker?"

"We're all the bee's knees down here. The Pres is still alive, I've only taken one round so far."

"Damn it, Knocker, are you hit?"

"Only a little bit. I'm fine, although the man's suit might have blood on it."

"Shit, shit, shit," Cara hissed as she swept her scope to the right to find the SAS man. When she located him, he was on his knees, his buttocks resting on his heels. His 416 was up and firing, but he was hunched over slightly. "Where are you hit?"

"Back, just to the side of my armor plate."

Cara thought for a moment. She couldn't call Brick because he was with Kane, which left Rucker, and he was in the middle of the buzz saw, working on other fallen operators.

"Rucker, you copy?"

"Send, Cara."

"Knocker's hit. I think it might be bad."

"I'm sorry, but I'm kind of tied up at the minute."

"Roger."

She swept back to Knocker and saw him hunched over but still firing. Movement caught her eye as Rear Admiral Alex Joseph crawled toward both him and the President.

"You hit hard, son?" Joseph asked Knocker as the SAS man changed out a spent magazine.

"Been hit harder by my ex-wife," he replied. "You want to get my friend here out of the way?"

"In case you haven't noticed—"

"Yeah, I know, there's a shitstorm all around us."

"Lie down and let me look at that wound," Joseph told him.

"Shit, if I lie down, I won't get back up. Just take the knife, cut the material, and have a look while I'm kneeling here. I've got—"

Knocker cursed and took a package out of one of his pouches. "Here, it's a dressing pack."

Bullets fizzed around them as Joseph looked at the wound. "There's no exit hole, son."

"Just plug it and I'll keep working."

"Yeah, of course you will."

The situation was dire. There were four wounded on the battlefield, and they were pinned down. Striker and Anvil were attempting to flank on the right while Kane, Axe, and Brick were going for the left flank. God only knew how bad the casualties were.

The President was still in danger, and Hank Jones, along with Alex Joseph, was on the firing line. What else could go wrong?

Twenty Thousand Feet Above the Battlefield

Arenas tested his parachute buckles and then made sure the SAW was secure, along with the spare ammunition. He looked at Traynor, who also was ready to go. When he saw that the operators on the ground were pinned down, Arenas had gone to Ferrero with a solution. He and Traynor would drop behind them and hit them from the rear.

Once more the ramp on the C-17 lowered, and two more men shuffled toward the rear. On reaching the end of the solid mass, they fell into nothingness.

On the Ground

Arenas felt like he'd been run over by a car, while Traynor felt no better. They knew when they jumped that there were no LZs close to where they needed to be, so they'd made the decision to put down in the trees. That presented no end of possibilities, one being the chance of them getting hung up or breaking limbs on their way through the canopy. Well, they had broken many limbs on the way down, just not their own, however much it felt like they did when they reached the ground.

Arenas looked at Traynor. "You're bleeding, *amigo.*"

"I'm not the only one."

Arenas reached for his comms. "Zero, this is Zero-One, over."

"Read you Lima Charlie, Zero-One."

"We're down and all good. Moving to target. Out."

"Roger, out."

"Reaper One, this is Zero-One, copy?"

"Copy, Zero-One."

"Reaper, Bravo Two and I are on the ground. We're closing on tangos' position from the rear."

"Roger that. Be careful. Out."

Kane was surprised by the news. To be in the position they were, they would have had to drop into the trees. Not a smart choice for your health, but in cases like this, you did what you had to do.

Besides, he couldn't worry about that right now. At present, they were trying to roll up the flank of their attackers. However, their opponents were experienced operators. They'd placed a machine gun on the flank where they were, and Kane figured they had done the same on the opposite one.

A line of bullets stitched along a mound in front of where Kane lay, sending up small geysers of earth. "Axe, put some fire on that bastard."

The SAW opened up, and a stream of outgoing rounds cut the air within the forest.

Beside him, Brick kept up a steady rate of fire with his 416 until his magazine ran dry. He rolled onto his back, replaced the empty with a fresh one, and opened fire once more.

"Reaper Three, copy?" Kane said as he pressed his transmit button.

"Copy," came the grunted reply.

"Give me a sitrep, Knocker."

"We're fucking pinned down and taking casualties. That's our fucking situation. If something doesn't happen soon, we're all fucking screwed."

Kane bristled at the reply, but there was something in the SAS man's voice that told him all was not right. "Cara, copy?"

"Got you, Reaper One."

"Can you get a line on Reaper Three?"

"What's up?"

"I want to know his situation."

"He's wounded, and Joseph is working on him while he's kneeling over the President."

"Shit. What else?"

"We've got battle casualties. The others are pinned down. I did see Striker and Anvil flanking opposite."

"We've run into a damned machine gun on our flank. I'd bet my left one that there's one on the other side too. They've set up good, but they're in for a surprise. Carlos and Traynor are on the ground and coming in from the east. They should be ready to engage soon."

"It needs to be sooner rather than later, or we're going to lose more people."

The pain radiating from the wound in Knocker's back was getting worse by the minute, not at all helped by the ministrations of Alex Joseph as he tried to dress it. Knocker looked down at the President, who lay face down with his hands over his head. "Hey, you still alive?"

Nelson nodded.

"Good," the SAS man growled against the pain. "Don't you worry about this. Ol' Knocker will get you out safe and…fucking hell, Admiral, are you trying to kill me before the mission is complete?" There were tears in the Brit's eyes, put there by the sharp tearing pain he'd just experienced.

"I thought you SAS guys were supposed to be tough?" Joseph inquired as a round snapped past his head.

"I know one thing, Admiral. If that helicopter wasn't where it was, we'd be dead by now."

As it happened, the helicopter was blocking some of the incoming fire. But they couldn't be lucky all the time, as the wound in Knocker's side had already proven.

However, the incoming fire was partially suppressed by the outgoing. Even though they were pinned down, the operators still managed to get a good amount out.

But the law of averages wasn't with the Brit this day, as he soon found out when two more rounds reached out and touched him. The first he took in his chest armor, the second in his leg. He grunted and fell forward. For a moment, Joseph thought he was dead, but a moan escaped Knocker's lips. Then he heard, "Fucking cock."

Arenas and Traynor could hear the automatic weapon fire clearly now. They were crouched and weaving their way through the tall pines. Between them and the shooters' firing line was a low ridge to which they bellied up. Once they crested, they saw the shooters well spread out, with light machine guns on each flank. They could see some of the wounded and dead behind the line being attended to. Whoever these guys were, they were professional.

"We need to take out the machine guns on each flank," Arenas said. "If we do, their flanks can be rolled up, and they'll have to pull out. The problem with that is there'll be nowhere for them to go."

Arenas settled down behind the SAW, and Traynor did the same with his 416. "Let me know when you're ready, Carlos."

Arenas sighted on the shooter with the light machine gun on his assigned flank and said, "Do it."

They opened fire and poured a hailstorm of bullets on the two machine gun positions, which immediately fell quiet. With those shooters killed or wounded, Arenas switched to targets of opportunity and went to work.

———————

When Arenas opened fire with the SAW, Brewer knew they were in trouble. The machine guns on their flank went quiet, then their position was raked from behind. The main problem was that with the flanks now open, they could be hit hard and forced back.

He turned to the man on his right—his second in command, a man named Ross—and said, "We just lost the initiative. We need to pull back and regroup."

"We're screwed, and you know it," Ross growled. "Our flanks are compromised, and they've got a strongpoint behind us. There's only one thing we *can* do."

"What's that?"

Ross raised his weapon and shot him in the head. "Cut and run."

He opened his coat, withdrew the envelope given to him by Clarissa, placed it on Brewer's body, and then said into his comms, "Fall back. Get out any way you can. We're done here."

The firing across the meadow died and an eerie silence enveloped the area, punctuated only by the moans of the wounded and the cursing of Master Chief Grady Ruggles. At her position on the low ridge, Cara rose to her feet. Was it really over?

"No one is shooting at me, so that's a good sign," she breathed. "All callsigns, check in."

"Reaper One, OK."

"Reaper Four, OK."

"Reaper Five, OK."

Silence.

"Reaper Three, check in."

Nothing.

"Knocker, check in, damn it."

The ensuing silence began to worry Cara. "If you don't—"

"Sod off, I hurt."

Cara smiled. "At least you're still alive. How's the President?"

"Better than I am."

"All right. I'll be there in a moment."

As she walked across the open ground, she assessed the situation. They were fortunate that they had not lost anyone, although they weren't in great shape. Joseph had used his influence to radio for a medevac. Kane and Axe were checking the dead and wounded from Brewer's team, and Brick was helping Rucker.

When she found Knocker, he was lying on his side, body armor and webbing discarded. Joseph was still with him, and Cara could see he had bloody hands. President Nelson sat beside them with his remaining Secret Service man. "Wow, Knocker, you're getting the Admiralty to look after you."

"Shut up. Let me die in peace."

"I think you'll survive," she said and looked at

Joseph.

"Medevac will be here soon, Cara," he assured her.

"Wait." It was the President. He stared at her curiously. "You're the one."

Cara frowned. "Sir?"

"The one who shot Frank."

"Frank, sir?"

"He was part of my detail. I know because I heard your man tell you to."

Cara realized he was talking about the man Knocker had warned her about. "Yes, sir. He was pulling a weapon."

"He would have shot me, so thank you."

"You need to thank Knocker, sir," she said, nodding at the SAS man. "He was the one who picked it up, and he used himself to shield you from those who wanted to kill you."

"Yes, you're right."

Cara looked at Jones and saw that Kane had returned and was talking to him. She hurried over and Kane said, "We found something."

Jones said, "I'll get the President."

"What is it?" she asked Kane

"Come with us and I'll show you." He looked at where Knocker lay. "How is he?"

"I'm not sure. I guess we'll know more when the medevac gets here."

Jones and Nelson joined them, along with the

remaining Secret Service agent. Kane led them into the tree line, where Axe waited for them. Kane pointed at a body on the ground. "That's Paul Brewer."

Nelson frowned. "CIA Director Paul Brewer?"

"Yes, sir. He's one of the Cabal lieutenants under Clarissa Rhodes," Jones told him. "All this was to kill you and us, Mister President, because we know too much. We have a list of names pointing at a whole bunch of Cabal people. His name wasn't on it, but he was involved with the thing at Incirlik. We also traced money to accounts, and we found out who Ares was."

"Yes, you told me that. It is Clarissa."

"No, the original Ares."

"What do you mean?"

Jones said, "Until recently, the Cabal remained in the shadows. Then we, or rather Mary, drew them out into the light. They didn't like that much and reacted accordingly. They murdered Melissa Smith, tried to kill me, and tried to flood the US with poisoned cocaine just to start a war with Colombia for a metal worth billions of dollars. Eventually, we worked out who it was, and we couldn't do a thing about it because no one would believe us. Then they brought the fight to us and assassinated Ares, framing me for it."

Nelson realized what Jones was saying. "Carter? You're saying Carter was this Ares?"

"Yes, sir. But like I said, they killed him and inserted Clarissa in his place."

"Good grief." Nelson paled.

"What is it, sir?"

"They played me, and I fell for it. Her, Brewer, Winkler."

"Winkler was on the list too, sir."

Kane cleared his throat, and they turned to him. "What is it?" Jones asked.

"Brewer had some things on him that pointed to him being Ares."

"He what? Show me."

Axe handed over what had been planted on the body and waited for Jones to read it. The general looked up and shook his head. "I don't understand."

"It's obviously a setup. He was shot at close range."

"How can you tell?" Nelson asked.

"I've been doing this for a long time. I can tell. There were a number of others the same way." He looked at Jones. "They killed their wounded."

The President shook his head. "This changes things. I need more evidence. All this does is point at Brewer being who you say Clarissa is."

"Trust me, sir," Jones said. "Our intel is good."

"I believe you, General, but I need evidence."

"Will you at least pull the troops out of Ukraine, sir?"

Nelson thought about it for a moment and nodded. "All right. I'll reach out to the Russian president and see if we can come to an agreement."

"Thank you, sir. I guess now I'm in your hands."

This time the thought process lasted longer. "No, I need you as my chairman."

Jones was stunned. "You—"

"That's what I said."

"Would you mind if I brought a few friends along until this is sorted out?"

"That won't be a problem," Nelson agreed.

"Also, the team—"

"Yes, yes, and I'll reinstate Alex as well."

"Alex, sir?"

"Yes, I told him after this was over that I wanted his resignation, but the next President will need good people around them."

"Are you resigning, Mister President?"

"I am. There's no point in waiting around for the inquiry. I'm done. This happened on my watch, and I enabled it. As soon as it's cleaned up, I'm gone."

"I'm sad to hear that. But before that happens, might I make a suggestion as to who you might want to put into the chair at the CIA?"

Nelson shrugged. "Why not? I can only say no. Who?"

"Alex Joseph."

"He's a sailor."

"He's a damned good man, and he's trustworthy," Jones growled.

"I'll think about it. If I move him, I'll need someone to take over NAVSPECWARCOM."

"I'll find you someone."

"We'll see what happens."

Nelson and his one-man Secret Service detail headed back to the LZ. Normally he would have been evacuated, but the helicopter had so many holes in it that the pilot thought it best not to fly.

Jones looked at Kane. "It's been a hell of a day, Reaper."

"Yes, sir. It sure has."

Washington, DC

"The mission was a bust," the voice on the other end said.

"Did you do what you had to?"

"Yes."

"Get your people as far away as possible."

"Already on our way."

"What about those left behind?"

"Taken care of. No one will talk or be traced back."

"Thank you for your devotion to the cause."

The call ended, and Clarissa sat back in her chair. This was it. Game over. The Cabal leaders across the globe were dead, killed by Thurston and her team, and the plan called for her to hold her nerve and stay the course. Everything pointed at Brewer; she'd made sure of that. They could rebuild. They had the money to do so.

There was a knock on her door, and a tall, thin man entered. "It's time to go, ma'am."

"I'll be right there, Stephen."

"Yes, ma'am."

"Stephen?"

"Yes, ma'am?"

"Is Michael with you today?"

"No, ma'am. It's the new guy you put on last week. Michael is off today."

"Thank you. I'll be with you shortly."

CHAPTER 20

Worldwide Drug Initiative HQ, El Paso, Texas
One Week Later

"In its daily press briefing, the White House told reporters that there is still no sign of House Speaker Clarissa Rhodes. It's been a week since she disappeared without a trace, and it has authorities worried about her safety. All this comes after bizarre reports of an attempt on President Richard Nelson's life which the press can't verify, other than to say that it came from off-the-record sources."

Kane flicked the television off and tossed the remote on the sofa beside him in the team's rec room. He sighed and closed his eyes, sheer exhaustion enveloping him. Sometimes it took him a few days to recover and get back to normal after a hard mission. This time, however, it seemed to be taking substantially longer.

"No sign of her yet?" Thurston asked from behind Kane.

He turned to look at her and wondered how long she'd been standing there. "Not yet. My gut says she's dead."

"Mine too," Thurston agreed as she came around to sit beside Kane. As she lowered herself, she gave a slight wince. The bruising on her face was fading slowly, and the rest of her body was starting to heal.

"Still hurting, huh?"

"Like you wouldn't believe."

"Have you heard anything about Knocker?"

"Doc Morales says he's driving everyone crazy at the hospital. The way he's recovering, she thinks they'll be back in Texas in another week."

"Can we get her to keep him there for another two?"

Thurston chuckled and winced. "Asshole. Don't make me laugh."

The sound of multiple footsteps came from behind them and Kane said, "Can't anyone get a moment's rest around here?"

"Harden up, princess," Cara said as she sat on the sofa beside him. Ferrero and Traynor found places on two recliners, while Swift stood with an excited expression on his face. "What is it?" Thurston asked the tech. "Tell me before you explode and we are all left wearing your innards."

"I managed to track down the accounts the Cabal was using and have frozen them all, but I found something while I was doing it."

"What's that?"

"Someone has been using them."

"Who?"

"I don't know. The transactions were made in Europe."

"Where was it accessed from?"

"The last time they were accessed was today, just before I froze them."

"Where, Slick?"

"A bank in Geneva."

"A bank?" Kane asked, sitting forward. "Did you get any stills from security cameras?"

"Yes."

Thurston asked, "Do you think it was Clarissa Rhodes?"

Swift shook his head. "Whoever it was knew about the cameras, so I wasn't able to get a shot of her face."

"It was a woman?"

"Yes."

"So, it could have been Clarissa Rhodes."

He shook his head. "No, that's just it. I was able to access medical records for Clarissa Rhodes. The person at the bank was too tall."

Thurston looked at Kane. "You know what this means, don't you?"

"Yeah. This thing isn't over. The Cabal is still out

there somewhere."

Potomac River, Washington, DC

The red and blue lights danced on the surrounding bushes while the bright lights of the tow truck shone to its rear, illuminating a black SUV that was not long out of the river. A detective started toward the vehicle, and as he approached it, he walked past a uniformed policeman. "What have we got?" he asked.

The uniform shook his head. "Two bodies. One in the front, one in the back. A man and a woman. Both were shot in the head."

"Shit," the detective moaned. "It's going to be a long night."

A LOOK AT: DEADLY WATER BY BRENT TOWNS AND SAM TOWNS

FROM THE AUTHOR OF THE ACTION-PACKED TEAM REAPER SERIES COMES A NEW PAGE-TURNER YOU WON'T WANT TO PUT DOWN!

A car bomb in a quiet suburban street sets in motion an investigation which will uncover the tentacles of organized crime stretching from the water-starved outback to the halls of power in the country's capital.

Senator Colin Worth was about to introduce a water bill which would cost the big producers millions before he was assassinated. However, the trail—as investigated by Detective Sergeant Gloria Browning and her team—only throws up more questions than answers.

Meanwhile, former undercover operative Dave Nash is brought in to investigate the disappearance of a water inspector in the town of Collari, on the Barwon River. But things take an even darker turn when Gloria's daughter, Rachel, is abducted.

Now, to get her back, Nash has to go against an organization who feeds its victims to the trees.

AVAILABLE NOW

ABOUT THE AUTHOR

A relative newcomer to the world of writing, Brent Towns self-published his first book, a western, in 2015. Last Stand in Sanctuary took him two years to write. His first hardcover book, a Black Horse Western, was published the following year. Since then, he has written a further 26 western stories, including some in collaboration with British western author, Ben Bridges.

Also, he has written the novelization to the upcoming 2019 movie from One-Eyed Horse Productions, titled, Bill Tilghman and the Outlaws. Not bad for an Australian author, he thinks.

He says, "The obvious next step for me was to venture into the world of men's action/adventure/thriller stories. Thus, Team Reaper was born."

A country town in Queensland, Australia, is where Brent lives with his wife and son.

For more information:
https://wolfpackpublishing.com/brent-towns/

Made in the USA
Las Vegas, NV
24 April 2021